Duckula and the
Haunted House

This book is dedicated to you out there – *whatever you are!*

Other books about Count Duckula from Carnival:

In the *Mini Hardback* series:
Vampire Vacation
Restoration Comedy
The Mystic Saxophone
The Ghost of Castle McDuckula

Novels:
Duckula on Treasure Island
Duckula and the Ghost Train Mystery
Duckula and the Haunted House

The Count Duckula Sticker Book

The Count Duckula Joke Book

The Count Duckula Storybook

JOHN BROADHEAD

Duckula and the Haunted House

CARNIVAL

Carnival
An imprint of the Children's Division
of the Collins Publishing Group
8 Grafton Street, London W1X 3LA

Published by Carnival 1989

Count Duckula is a registered trademark of
THAMES TELEVISION Plc.
Copyright © Cosgrove Hall Productions 1989

ISBN 0 00 194877 6

Printed and bound in Great Britain by
Collins, Glasgow

Set in Times

1
Wires 'n' Things!

The dark clouds which had hung over Castle Duckula all morning began to unleash a steady downpour of chill rain. In fact, it was a normal day in Transylvania!

Trudging his way up the long, winding path towards the Castle was a representative of the Transylvanian Stork Parcel Post Delivery Service. The poor, pitiful creature tried hard to keep a parcel safe in his large beak as he fought against the wind and rain. The grim outline of the Castle loomed closer. He trembled . . . with cold and also with trepidation. It's not fair! he thought. Nowhere in his job description did it mention calling on the most dreaded, most feared vampire in the land – Count Duckula!

C-r-e-a-k! The huge, heavy door opened just a fraction. The parcel was thrust into a waiting claw, and, if the terrified, breathless visitor hadn't turned and run away so fast, he might have been surprised to hear whoops of delight from inside the Castle.

'I've been waiting for this!' yelled Count Duckula, as he impatiently unwrapped the layers of brown paper.

Nanny was almost as excited! 'Oooh, a parcel!' she cried. 'I loves gettin' a parcel through the post! I wonder what's in it?'

'I *know* what's in it,' said Duckula. 'My new electronics set! I sent for it from an advert in *The Transylvanian Electronic Weekly* magazine.'

Nanny looked slightly deflated, 'But, Duckyboos, if you knows what it is, then it's not a surprise. Parcels through the post are much nicer if they're a surprise.'

'Nanny! If I didn't know what it was, how could I have sent for it in the first place?' blurted Duckula. Nanny did say some exasperating things at times. Actually, she said exasperating things all the time!

At last, the brightly coloured box was revealed! On the lid was printed "The Young Electronics Enthusiast's First Set'.

Inside was an amazing array of tiny switches and bulbs, little pieces of wire, transistors, circuit boards and lots more fascinating bits and pieces.

Nanny stared, a bewildered expression on her plump face. 'Duckyboos, it's all twiddly bits o' wire an' things. What a cheek they've got, sending you that mess instead of your elec . . . electricky set or whatever it was you wanted.'

'But this is exactly what I want!' replied Duckula.

'Er, hmm, excuse me, milord,' coughed Igor the butler, trying to catch his young master's attention. 'I . . . er . . . I'm sorry to introduce a note of reality, but how do you propose to pay for this . . . this amusement?'

Duckula scowled. Trust Igor to put a damper on things! 'It's all sorted out, Igor,' he said. 'I'm paying by instalments . . . easy payments . . . credit. Haven't you ever heard of such arrangements?'

'Indeed I have, sir,' replied Igor. 'I just hope you haven't overstretched your finances. Now overstretching a guest or two on the rack down in the dungeon . . . now that's a different matter entirely!'

'Igor!! None of that gruesome stuff, please!'

'Sorry, milord. I was overcome.'

'You will be, if you keep talking like that. You know I don't like it.' Duckula held up a note which was inside the parcel. 'Listen to this,' he said in a serious manner. 'It explains how much I've got to pay. Here's what it says: "terms are 100 weekly payments of 25 Transylvanian drachmas."'

Igor's face turned an even ghastlier colour than usual. 'But milord, that's a total price of 2,500 drachmas.'

'Oh . . . er, if you say so,' agreed Duckula, irritated. Mental arithmetic wasn't his strong point. Why did Igor always have to be so boring? 'I happen to think the price is very reasonable, so there!' he told his butler.

'Maybe, milord,' said Igor, 'but could I venture to ask how you propose to raise such a sum?'

'Really, Igor! The whole idea is that I don't need to raise such a sum. I merely raise the weekly sum.'

'But milord, I fear you fail to appreciate how low the castle coffers are.'

'Are you saying we're broke?'

'Let me put it like this, milord: even one week's instalment would stretch the Castle budget right now. Oh, dear me, there I go again, talking about stretching. Er, perhaps we might raise a little money by showing curious visitors around the dungeons?'

'And then stretching them on the rack?' continued Duckula. 'Igor, I'm getting fed up with your attitude. You are so ghoulish!'

'Thank you, milord,' replied Igor sincerely.

Nanny, who'd been busy examining the strange jumble of wires, gave her opinion. 'I thinks you should send it back, Duckyboos. You couldn't do anything with it. It's all broke, with the wires stickin' out.'

'I most certainly *could* do something with it!' yelled the angry little Count. 'I intend to make all kinds of clever gadgets that do all kinds of clever things!'

All the same, Igor's news about the sorry state of the Castle finances worried Duckula. He'd no idea they were so hard-up; but then he rarely concerned himself with such matters! And he was determined to keep his precious electronics set. I won't send it back, he thought, I just won't!

After a while, Duckula cheered up. It wasn't in his nature to be gloomy for very long. He'd made up his mind to pursue his new hobby and become a dab-hand at electronics, and to do that, he needed his electronics set, come what may. It was as simple as that – and he usually got his own way in the end!

Anyway, the bright spot of the day was about to begin: the Transylvanian *Open Polytechnic* TV programme – on electronics, of course!

Duckula switched on the TV and settled down to watch. Having his very own electronics set would make the programme even more interesting! And some refreshments would make it nicer still!

'Nanny, how about some broccoli sandwiches and a banana milkshake?' he called.

'Can't do a milkshake, Duckyboos,' called Nanny. 'The milkman wouldn't leave extra pints 'cos we owe him for three weeks. I'll make you a nice cup o' tea instead.'

Really! This was too bad, thought Duckula. Here he was, supposed to be a Count living in a Castle on a mountaintop, and he couldn't even afford a measly milkshake!

'Even the TV doesn't work properly,' he groaned, twiddling with the knobs. It was an old set; in fact, it was one of the very oldest still working!

At last, the ancient set spluttered into life and an announcer appeared on the screen. The lunchtime news was just ending and the announcer was saying, 'Now for a final news item. Windup Manor is said to be one of Britain's most haunted houses and the owners, Lord and Lady Windup, are too scared to live in their ancestral home.

'The editor of the popular newspaper the *Daily Gossip* is offering a prize of £1,000 to anyone who can spend a whole night in the Manor. The newspaper thinks it's a shame that His Lordship, who is ninety-nine years old, has been forced out.

'Once Lord and Lady Windup are satisfied that there are no ghosts in the house, they will be willing to return. Lady Windup will then be able to carry on with the project that has taken her many years and eaten up most of the Windup fortune: to turn part of the grounds of Windup Manor into a Gardenarium – Her Ladyship's term for a nature reserve for rare trees, plants and flowers.'

'Hey!' Duckula sat up in his chair. 'A thousand pounds! What's that in drachmas . . .? It's – it's a whole lot, anyway! Igor! Nanny! Here's how we can make enough money to pay for my electronics set *and* have lots left over!'

9

2

Manners and Cabbages!

Igor and Nanny weren't very impressed by Duckula's plan. That was to be expected, of course. Sometimes he felt like sacking them both and hiring servants who shared his sense of adventure. But then, what would he do without Nanny's cocoa? Making cocoa was one of the few things she was good at!

As for Igor . . . well, Igor was so pathetically servile – and he was also occasionally useful for getting Duckula out of scrapes. All right, he was morbid and dull and hankered after the old days when he served Duckula's ancestors, but where could you find such a faithful butler these days?

'It all sounds like a cheap publicity stunt to me,' was Igor's first comment.

'Of course it's a publicity stunt!' exclaimed Duckula. 'Not so cheap though . . . at a thousand pounds! It's great publicity for Lord Whatsisname. He probably wants to attract tourists to the place!'

'I wonder if he has a dungeon ready for them?' pondered Igor.

'Igor, don't start all that again. Listen, I'm going to ring that newspaper right now!'

'Ooh, Duckyboos, please don't,' pleaded Nanny. 'I 'ates ghosts an' monsters an' spooks an' things.'

'Nanny, there are no such things!'

'But there's vampires.'

'Yes, there's vampires. Hey, wait a minute – I'm a vampire, unfortunately!'

'I know, Duckyboos . . . so if there's vampires, there could be ghosts an' monsters.'

'On this occasion, Nanny's argument does seem to possess a certain logic,' said Igor. 'I happen to believe that many evil creatures are lurking around old houses.'

'Well, I don't believe it!' snapped Duckula, picking up the phone. 'Hello! Operator? Put me through to the *Daily Gossip*, please.'

The next week was a very busy one in the Duckula household, with lots of packing and planning to be done.

'I'm makin' sure you've got all your warm undies,' said Nanny. 'It'll be cold in that 'aunted house.'

'Don't fuss, Nanny,' retorted Duckula, as he struggled to perfect his Electronic Ghost Repeller. 'Listen to this!'

He pushed a button on an odd-looking contraption, causing it to give out an ear-piercing shriek!

Nanny covered her ears. 'What a terrible noise, Duckyboos. It's enough to scare any monsters.'

'Ah! Just as I thought!' cried Duckula. 'No ghosts will get a look-in when I'm around – er, not that I believe in such things anyway!'

Everything was ready! It was time to set off in the age-old way that Duckula and his ancestors had always travelled: by Castle! How the Castle was set in motion was a great mystery, known only to the current master – and sometimes Duckula didn't get it exactly right!

'Hold on . . . here we go!' called Duckula, as he climbed into the ancient, upright sarcophagus, there to say the magic words which would whisk the enormous Castle from the bleak, desolate mountaintop in the Transylvanian Alps to the green grass of the English countryside.

Bump! The Castle landed – hopefully in the right place, thought Duckula! The three travellers emerged to find themselves in lush parkland. Nearby stood a tiny, very pretty cottage, complete with roses round the door.

'Good! We've landed right on target!' exclaimed Duckula.

And so they had; which made a welcome change from other times! When the Castle had ended up on Blackpool beach instead of in the Sahara Desert, for instance, and when it had landed on top of a banana tree instead of in the Bahamas!

Nanny liked the cottage. 'What a nice little house! It doesn't look a bit like it's 'aunted!'

'I must admit to some disappointment, milord,' remarked Igor. 'This house is sickeningly . . . quaint!'

'This isn't the haunted house!' explained Duckula. 'It's the gamekeeper's cottage, where we meet Lord Windup. He should be in; he's expecting us.'

Duckula knocked on the door, which then opened very slightly.

'Mister Duckula?' The voice was a low, gruff whisper.

'Count Duckula, if you please!'

'Suit yourself. You'd better come in, I suppose.' The door opened wider to reveal a fellow who looked like a large magpie – dressed as a butler, but very shabbily. His face was mean and his eyes shifty.

Duckula entered the house, followed by Igor and Nanny. The butler pulled an extremely grubby handkerchief from his pocket. He unfolded it to reveal a mass of sticky sweets, all stuck together in a horrible mess.

'Like one?' he asked Duckula.

'Er, no thanks,' replied Duckula hastily, thinking he'd rather eat Nanny's custard . . . lumps and all!

'Please yourself,' shrugged the butler. 'I'm having one anyway. They must 'ave been in this pocket for about six months. I forgot about 'em!' Then, with a mighty tug, he pulled a single sweet free from the rest and popped it in his mouth. 'Mmmm, tastes nice,' he declared, proceeding to suck a couple more! 'They've matured and improved with age! Can't say the same about His Lordship!'

'Where is Lord Windup?' asked Duckula.

'Over there,' mumbled the butler through a mouthful of sticky sweets, gesturing in the general direction of an armchair.

Sure enough, Lord Windup was sitting bolt upright in the chair: fast asleep and snoring loudly. By his side was a stout walking stick.

'Milord,' hissed Igor, irritated. 'You haven't introduced Nanny and me to this . . . this uncouth servant.'

'Oh, by the way,' said Duckula, 'this is Igor, my butler and this is my Nanny.'

'So what?' grunted the creature. 'They're nothing to show off about . . . I'd sack 'em, if I were you!'

13

Igor bristled with anger and Nanny nearly exploded! How dare this untidy butler say such things!

'I trust you are His Lordship's butler?' Igor's tone was cold as ice.

'You trust right, mate. Mitch Manners is the name, not that it's any of your business.'

'In my day, a butler knew his place,' said Igor.

'*You'll* know your place in a minute, you ugly old stuffed shirt!' replied Manners.

'Don't you insult Mr Igor,' cried Nanny. ''e may be ugly, but his shirt's not stuffed. Now peppers, they can be stuffed. I saw it done in a cookery programme on TV.'

'What's the old hen talkin' about?' sneered Manners. 'Shut her up before she blows a fuse.'

'Who's there? Halt! Halt, I say! Take that . . . and that!' Lord Windup had woken with a sudden start and was lashing about wildly with his stick. Nanny was closest to the old man's chair and unfortunately her wide expanse of flesh made a convenient landing place!

'Ouch!' she yelled, as the stick made contact.

Poor Duckula was dumbfounded! Had they come all this way to be insulted and beaten with sticks?

'It's all right, Guv'', said Manners to his master. 'This lot won't cause us any trouble. They've come down to stay at the big house. That little 'un . . . he calls himself a Count.'

'I *am* a Count!' Duckula was very indignant. 'And yes . . . I have come to meet the challenge and stay

14

the night in the haunted house because I don't believe in ghosts!'

Lord Windup spluttered, shedding a cloud of loose feathers. 'You *will* believe, me boy! You *will*! Once you've had experiences like I've had! Why, a ghost it was who stole me gold watch; snatched it from right under me nose as I wound it up! That was enough for me, I can tell you! Dashed annoying! Poor Lady Windup, she's heartbroken. Wanted to start some kind of botanical thing in the grounds, you know. Had it all planned out, spent a fortune on it . . . but, well, since these spooks moved in, she's had to forget all that.'

A tiny face on the end of a long, long neck peered out from behind the chair. 'Yoo-hoo . . .!' The voice reminded Nanny of the whistling kettle in the Castle kitchen.

'Come out, me dear,' bellowed Lord Windup. 'They're not ghosts!'

Lady Windup emerged from behind the chair. She had large eyes, a thin, sharp beak and long spindly legs.

'Ooh, I'm so pleased you're not ghosts,' she whined, extending her hand. 'I'm so very displeased at the ghosts for preventing my wonderful plans. Why we should be troubled with ghosts, I really don't know. What have we done to deserve them, I ask myself. I was going to introduce several species of endangered vegetables this year . . .'

It was clear that, once Lady Windup started talking, it was hard to stop her, but Nanny managed it by making an effort to curtsey.

'Pleased to meet you, Your Ladyship,' she said, as she went down . . . and down . . . and down!

Everyone gasped as Nanny lost her balance and toppled sideways onto what looked like a gigantic potted plant.

Lady Windup screamed and ran forward. Her concern wasn't for Nanny but for the plant! 'My South American Red-Flowered Spotted Cabbage!' she cried. 'Is it all right? It's so rare and delicate . . .'

Duckula thought the horrid vegetable looked about as delicate as Nanny! Even a vegetarian like himself who loved ordinary cabbage wouldn't fancy eating a plateful of this strange variety!

'They've stolen all sorts o' things . . . even me stomach powders!' rambled Lord Windup, oblivious to the desperate struggle to pull Nanny from the now squashed spotted cabbage.

'Who have?' gasped Duckula.

'The spooks, of course!' bellowed Lord Windup.

'I see,' said Duckula. The old boy was obviously dotty!

Free now, Nanny flopped down on a sofa. 'Can't we go 'ome. Duckyboos? What with funny cabbages and thievin' spooks, I've gone all shivery.'

'That's because you're sitting on a cold hot-water bottle, Nanny,' sighed Igor.

'Oh, so I am, Duckyboos! An' it's burst!'

'I wondered where me water bottle had got to,' said Lord Windup.

'Anyway, I *still* don't believe in ghosts,' declared Duckula.

This angered Manners, who sneered, 'His Lordship

isn't a fibber. What he says is true. Why, he can't even live in his own ancestral home any more 'cos of them spooks. There's the one that rattles the chains, the one that walks with his head under his arm, the one in the long white cloak, the one in the suit of armour, the one . . .'

'I think we've got the picture!' Duckula had heard enough!

Suddenly, the door burst open and there was a blinding flash.

'Smile please! Say "cheese!"' called a chirpy voice.

It was Sandy Swift, ace reporter and photographer from the *Daily Gossip*. 'How about an interview, Mr Ducktail?' he asked cheerily.

A squeaky voice rang out from behind the reporter. 'There's not much time for interviews. It's nearly Lord Windup's bedtime!'

It was a small cuckoo of a man with merry, twinkling eyes and dressed in some kind of servant's outfit. He had bits of dust and cobwebs all over him, as if he'd been scrambling around in an old attic or cellar.

'Hello! I'm Good-Time Charlie, the footman,' he grinned, holding up a pair of carpet slippers. 'I've brought your slippers from the big house, milord.'

How strange to get so dusty looking for slippers, thought Duckula. Still Lord Windup seemed so eccentric, perhaps he kept his slippers up the chimney!

17

3
All Alone?

Sandy Swift, the cheeky newspaper reporter promised to be quick . . . and he certainly lived up to his name! He was like a living whirlwind – taking picture after picture and asking question after question. The furiously popping flashbulbs in his camera made Duckula blink and Igor very uncomfortable. Igor much preferred the gloom, anyway!

As for Nanny, well, she was very pleased to be having her picture taken, but wished she'd put her feathers in curlers first! Lord Windup continued to wave his stick around at anyone who came near and Manners just kept telling the reporter to 'clear off!'

Then, with a great deal of noise and commotion, the television reporters arrived. Lights were quickly set up around the tiny sitting room and within a few minutes a smartly dressed, well-known television personality was facing the camera and saying:

'We've come down to Windup Manor, said to be the country's most haunted house. This modest little place isn't the Manor, of course, but the gamekeeper's cottage. We're here to meet the courageous Count Duckula, who, true to his noble background, has volunteered to spend the night alone, braving those legendary spooks and ghouls.'

'Oooh, Duckyboos, we're on TV!' cooed Nanny.

A microphone was pushed under Duckula's beak.

'Count Duckula, what made you want to take on this challenge? Was it purely and simply the money . . . or, as we all suspect, do you have other, loftier motives?'

Duckula preened himself. It was quite pleasant being a celebrity! 'Er, yes . . . it was the money, of course. But not *just* the money. I want to prove that there's no need to be scared of ghosts, because they don't exist!'

'I see, Count Duckula. But just supposing you do meet a spook, what will you do?'

Igor decided to have his say. 'Rest assured! My master, who is descended from the venerated Duckula line, is more than a match for any feeble ghost.'

'Even so, Count Duckula,' continued the reporter, 'it's very brave of you to stay all night in that place – absolutely and completely alone!'

'Well, nice of you to say so. I guess I am quite brave. Hey, wait a minute – who said anything about alone? I won't be *all* alone, will I?'

This was Sandy Swift's cue to push forward. 'Why yes, of course Count Ducktail is spending the night all alone in the dreaded haunted house!' Sandy looked cheerier than ever, as he explained Duckula's unenviable situation. 'It's an express condition of the agreement. I mean to say, we can't make much of a story of it otherwise, can we?'

'C . . . an't we?' spluttered a suddenly not-so-brave Duckula. 'But I never go anywhere without my butler and my Nanny . . .'

The television reporter took over, hastily moving on to the history of Windup Manor and how poor

19

Lord and Lady Windup were too scared out of their wits to live in the old place any more and were thinking about selling it, although they didn't want to because of Lady Windup's exciting and revolutionary thinking on vegetables.

He seemed to say all this without stopping for breath . . . and finished up by explaining how even selling the house would prove difficult, as the extremely ancient deeds had disappeared. 'Probably stolen by a spook!' he grinned, showing lots of white teeth.

Duckula was glad when the television cameras had gone. 'OK, maybe I'm *not* supposed to have anyone with me,' he grumbled to Igor. 'But you and Nanny don't count, surely!'

'Duckyboos, what a fib!' blurted Nanny. 'I can count! One, two, three, four . . . er . . . six. And Mr Igor can count up to about 'undred.'

Duckula turned to Sandy the reporter. 'See what I mean? Having Nanny with me in a haunted house would be more of a liability than a safeguard. Anyway, I *am* a Count and I should be allowed to take my staff!'

Sandy shook his head. 'They can't go, Count Ducktail . . .'

Duckula grimaced. He was getting fed up correcting Sandy. 'For the last time! Count Duckula! I repeat, Count Duckula!'

'No Duckyboos, 'es not Count Duckula,' said Nanny. 'You're Count Duckula. You must be poorly, forgettin' who you are. 'Ere, let me feel your forehead . . .'

As Duckula dodged Nanny's attentions, he wondered if perhaps the ghosts would be less trouble after all!

Sandy continued. 'No, sorry, Count Duckpond! Your servants can't go with you. It's out of the question! Think of the readers: they want to be thrilled and terrified by your lone adventure without leaving the safety of their own armchairs!'

Duckula frowned. 'Never mind the readers. How how about me? And for the very, very last time, it's Count Duckula, if you don't mind!'

'I don't mind if you don't mind! Call yourself whatever you like. Of course, if you were a real aristocrat you wouldn't be putting yourself through this ordeal for a thousand pounds.'

Sandy's attitude was more than Igor could stand. Duckula might be penniless – or rather, drachmaless – but nevertheless he *was* a true Count. If there was one thing Igor would not tolerate, it was to have the noble line of Duckula, the name he had served for centuries, belittled.

'Let me assure you that my master is indeed a real Count – and he is taking on this challenge to demonstrate his immense bravery.'

Sandy was convinced. 'I see! Well, that makes it all the more interesting! A real Count, eh?'

'Indeed!' replied Igor. 'And far from being afraid of staying in the house alone, Master Duckula prefers it. Indeed, he *insists* on it!'

'Yes, I do!' beamed Duckula, carried away for the moment by Igor's praises. 'Er . . . I do?'

Nanny clutched Duckula to her huge body. 'You

21

can't leave me poor little Duckyboos to those ghosts and monsters!'

'Nanny, don't fuss,' said Igor.

Lord Windup, who had been snoozing, woke up suddenly and lashed out with his stick, catching Nanny again.

'Ouch!' she cried.

'You're a hefty wench!' bellowed His Lordship. 'The new housemaid, are you? Don't think you'll be able to get through the kitchen door!'

'Nanny doesn't bother with doors, anyway!' chuckled Duckula.

'I look after Master Duckyboos,' said an indignant Nanny. 'I wouldn't want to work for you, not even if you paid me wages!' For just a fleeting moment, it occurred to her that she'd never had any wages from the Duckula household, something she'd been meaning to ask about for a century or two!

'Pity,' said Lord Windup. 'I can't get staff.'

Igor smiled wryly. Judging by Lord Windup's choice of butler, that much was very clear, he thought.

It was quite cosy with everyone piled into the little cottage. Duckula began to enjoy the limelight, as long as he didn't think about the haunted house! Nanny made tea in the tiny kitchen and produced a whole pile of coconut cakes from her sling.

Duckula settled down in a big armchair and almost dozed off to sleep. How nice it would be if he could simply collect the prize money without the bother of staying in the dreaded house!

'Can't find the deeds, you see!' The voice startled Duckula from his slumbers. It was Lord Windup, babbling on. 'Might be dashed difficult to sell a haunted house, you know. But I'm strapped for cash . . . and then there's me good lady's botanic garden . . . can't be done, can't be done . . .'

'Don't worry, milord,' said Manners. 'With all the publicity from this Duckula character, they'll be queuing up to buy the old dump, even if it *is* haunted! You'll be able to make a packet and the old girl can start her vegetable plot somewhere nice an' modern. Like those detached houses they're buildin' on that new estate. Smart, they are!'

'The house might be especially sought after if it does prove to be haunted,' piped up Sandy. 'It could become an exclusive hotel or country club. If Count Ducksoup does meet a spook, we can make a good story out of it!'

Nanny had an idea how Lord and Lady Windup could raise some cash. 'Take lodgers in!' she squawked.

'There are plenty of lodgers there already – spooky ones!' laughed the butler.

'We're in so much debt and the house needs extensive repairs,' explained Lady Windup. 'Such a pity. How I'd love to start my endangered vegetable sanctuary there, but it does look like we'll have to sell up.'

'Hate to part with the old place,' muttered Lord Windup. 'The family has lived there for generations.'

Igor sympathised with this sentiment. It was like Count Duckula having to leave Castle Duckula. Unthinkable!

'Anyone got the time?' asked Good-Time Charlie, whose every sentence seemed to be about time.

23

'Time this brainless duck went ghost-hunting!' said Manners with a cruel laugh.

'What? Oh, very good, Manners!' replied his master.

'Very *good* manners? Rather a poor description,' murmured Igor.

It was nearly midnight – the moment of truth! Time for Duckula to begin his night of . . . well, who knows what? The television and newspaper reporters were based in a caravan parked in the grounds of the big house. Lord and Lady Windup and his butler were still in the gamekeeper's cottage while Igor and Nanny settled down in the gardener's cottage next door.

All very cosy – except for poor Duckula who had to make his way to the Manor. Carrying his torch in one hand and his electronics set in the other, he trod fearfully through the tall trees towards the dark shape of the huge old house.

'Psst! Psst!'

The sound came from behind thick bushes. Then a figure stepped forward, slowly, steathily. Duckula almost froze with fright. Was it a ghost – already?

4

The Ghost Hunters

'Who – is – that?' gasped Duckula.

'I represent the *Daily Rag*,' came the reply. 'My editor's asked me to put a proposition to you.'

Duckula sighed with deep relief. The 'ghost' was just another newspaper reporter!

The voice continued. 'If you meet a real ghost and take a photograph of it, my paper will pay you double what the *Daily Gossip* is paying you for staying the night there!'

Duckula was utterly confused. 'But I don't expect to see a ghost. I don't believe in ghosts – see!'

'Aha! Hee, hee!' chuckled the dark figure of the reporter. 'You will . . . when you meet the headless knight, the hellish hound, the 'orrible abbot, the laughing lady, the mischievous monk, the spiteful spirit, the musical . . .'

'All right! All right!' yelled Duckula. 'You've convinced me!'

'Well, what d'you say?' hissed the newspaper fellow. 'D'you agree to take a picture of a spook? It'll make front page news and you'll make a lot of cash!'

'But . . . but I've made arrangements with the *Daily Gossip*. I signed a bit of paper.'

'Well, look at it this way: if you don't see a spook, then you get the money from the *Daily Gossip*, and if you do see one – tell it to say "cheese" and take a snap of it! That way you can't lose and you don't need to tell anyone any fibs.'

Duckula thought for a moment. It seemed to make sense. What seemed a better idea still was to abandon the whole crazy scheme – but it was too late for that. As well as being scared out of his wits, he was smarting with anger from not being able to take Igor and Nanny into the house with him. Naturally, he wanted fame and glory – not to mention the prize money! – for himself.

But he was an important aristocrat, or so Igor kept telling him. Surely, then, he could be excused for insisting that his butler and Nanny accompany him. It simply wasn't fair!

It was this line of thought that decided him to agree to the *Daily Rag*'s suggestion.

'OK. If I do see a ghost, I'll ask it to smile and take its picture. Hey, I haven't got a camera.'

The reporter thrust a small camera into Duckula's shaking hand. 'Use this. It's one of those self-developing cameras. You can see the photos in a few minutes. There's a powerful electronic flash too, so you can take pictures in the dark.'

'Electronic, eh?' Normally, Duckula would have been only too pleased at the prospect of using the camera, especially with electronic flash. But this wasn't a normal situation.

'I'll be off then. Good luck!' called the newspaper chap, as he disappeared into the night.

Duckula stood before the massive front door of Windup Manor. He felt very tiny. How he wished he could turn back. How he wished Nanny was here. He kept reminding himself of the money, but when you're standing on the doorstep of a haunted house . . . well, it's hard to think about anything else but ghosts. Bet you don't envy him, do you?

Very gingerly, he pushed the heavy door. It moved slowly and creakily, but at last it was open enough for him to slip through the gap.

'Phew!' breathed Duckula, relieved that he was inside and hadn't seen a ghost yet. Actually, he couldn't see very much at all, because it was so dark, and he'd put his torch in his pocket when he took hold of the camera. Foolish thing to do, he thought, as he felt in the big pocket of the overcoat Nanny had made him wear to keep warm. The silly coat was miles too big anyway and the pockets were full of holes . . . including the pocket where the torch should have been!

'Help!' The cry was almost silent. There was no one to hear. Alone, in the dead of night, in a haunted house – and without even a torch! Luckily, the pocket holding the broccoli sandwiches was intact!

Duckula wanted to be brave. Indeed, he knew he could be brave, when he had no alternative. Like the time he and Nanny and Igor got involved with pirates on a treasure island. But coping with ghosts and Nanny's silly rules about warm overcoats was too much for even the bravest of Vampire Counts. He stamped his feet in anger. 'Nanny! Just wait till I see you again!'

Then a terrible thought struck him. Would he survive this ordeal to see Nanny again? 'Oh . . . Nanny, I'm so miserable,' he whimpered. His only

27

other consolation – besides the sandwiches – was that his precious electronics set was still safe. He just hoped that the very clever ghost-repeller and early-warning spook system he'd made with it *worked*!

A rickety motorcar trundled its way through the countryside, up and down hills and along winding lanes.

'Tra-la la!' sang the driver to himself, happy in the knowledge that he was on his way to do what he liked doing best: ghost-hunting! He was a curious-looking individual: large and untidy with a huge bunch of bedraggled feathers covering his head, giving it the appearance of a sweeping brush. His name suited him, for this was none other than the famous psychical researcher, Professor Daftasa-Brush!

'Wake-up, Owlie,' he called to his companion, who was sleeping in the seat beside him. 'We'll soon be there!'

'What? *What*? Too-wit! Too-woo!' The passenger, one Professor Barn-Owl, renowned for his genius in just about everything, as well as in tracking down spooks, awoke from his slumbers, sat bolt upright, and began to talk rapidly. 'The square on the hypotenuse is equal to . . .'

'Oh, stop that, Owlie! We're nearly at Windup Manor!'

'I say, Dafty! How enthralling! What time is it?'

'Almost . . . oh dear, where's my watch?'

'Probably stuck in the feathers on your head, my dear fellow,' replied the other, knowing that this was

28

where his friend's lost belongings could usually be found.

Dafty shook his head and an old-fashioned watch and chain fell out. 'Must fasten it back onto my waistcoat,' he mumbled, adding that it was almost one o'clock in the morning of Midsummer's Day – when Windup Manor was said to be at its most haunted!

'Will we be able to gain access to this haunted abode?' asked the learned Barn-Owl.

'Of a certainty! The place is empty and unlocked. They say it's so haunted that the owner, Lord Windup, has abandoned it. Just think Owlie, if we can catch a ghost with our advanced electronic equipment, then we'll be the toasts of the scientific world. They'll *have* to take us seriously.'

'Quite so, Dafty. Quite so. Our combined hundred years' work on this subject will not have been in vain!'

Nanny was desolate. She sat by the window in the cottage, looking out at the night and wondering what was happening to her darling Duckula.

'It's not *right*, Mr Igor,' she complained. 'Making poor little Duckyboos stay all night in that 'orrible place all by 'imself.'

Igor, on the other hand, although he felt it was his duty to attend to his master's needs and protect him, couldn't fully share Nanny's concern. In fact, he was rather envious. The thought of spending the night in a house which was even more ghastly than Castle Duckula appealed to him. He had reservations about the existence of the supposed spooks, but the place had a deliciously decrepit and delightfully gloomy look about it. Ideal for a weekend break, he thought.

'Don't worry too much about the young master, Nanny. Even if the house is genuinely haunted, which I doubt, then a proud Duckula Vampire Count will surely put the wind up the miserable creatures! Oh . . . er, I rather think I made a *pun*, then, Nanny.'

'A pen, Mr Igor? You've made a *pen*? 'Ow clever you are! What are you goin' to write with it?'

Before Igor could answer, Nanny's attention was caught by something outside. 'Mr Igor, come 'ere, quick!' she called. 'There's a motorcar over there. I can see the lights. And two funny lookin' types are gettin' out of it.'

'Probably newspaper reporters,' sighed Igor. 'I suggest you stop fretting and go to bed, Nanny.'

'But they've got torches and they're creeping towards the 'aunted 'ouse. Ooh, Mr Igor, will they do Duckyboos any 'arm? Perhaps they're ghosts!'

'Ghosts in a motorcar? Really Nanny! Move away from the window and let me see.'

Igor looked . . . and he couldn't help but feel a slight concern. *Could* Duckula be in danger?

5
Let's Follow 'em!

Nanny was getting more and more agitated. She was very scared of ghosts and monsters and such like – but she'd tackle *anything* to protect her precious Duckula!

'Let's follow 'em, Mister Igor,' she whined. 'Whether they're ghosts or not, I'm sure they can't be up to no good.'

Igor, too, knew his duty. 'All right Nanny,' he agreed. 'We'll follow at a safe distance, but only to look after the master's interests, you understand.'

So out they crept into the dark, dark night. They tried to keep as quiet as mice when they passed the caravan where the reporters were, though judging by the loud snores coming from that direction, they needn't have worried. No wonder the two strangers in the motorcar hadn't attracted any media attention!

Duckula sat, shivering and miserable, inside the house. If he'd known how close by Igor and Nanny were, he might have felt better. He'd become used to the dark now, and fortunately, moonlight shone through some of the tall windows. Outside, a wind was getting up, whistling around the towers and turrets of the old house, blowing through the cracks in the doors and windows and down the chimney into the massive unlit hearth in the room where Duckula had ventured.

31

The young Count found his way to a big sofa, on which he snuggled up and closed his eyes. He hoped to fall asleep and wake to find it was morning. Of course, he had to remember that Castle Duckula always returns to Transylvania at dawn, Eastern Transylvanian time, so he'd have to be sure to collect his prize money before then. Or maybe they'd send it on; he yawned. There'd be TV interviews; he was so sleepy. In a few minutes he *was* asleep!

Professors Barn-Owl and Daftasa-Brush each had a secret which neither could confess to the other – or to anyone else, for that matter. They were both *afraid* of ghosts!

Not that either had ever actually met one yet, but if they did, there was a good chance that they'd turn and run a mile, which, for professional ghost-hunters, is rather a shameful state of affairs, don't you think?

Yet there they were, creeping through the slightly open door of a very haunted house! Past the sleeping Duckula they went, without even noticing him, although Professor Barn-Owl thought he heard something.

'Listen,' he whispered. 'What was that?'

'Sounds like snoring!' answered his companion.

'Just as I thought . . . the snoring spectre! First mentioned in *The Noises Spooks Make*, written by Doctor Scaredypants, the well-known authority on matters psychic.'

'Let's leave our highly sensitive, spooked-up tape-recorder here to catch the sounds,' suggested Professor Daftasa-Brush.

'Excellent idea!' agreed Professor Barn-Owl. 'Then we'll venture upstairs . . .'

Outside, Igor and Nanny were nearing the house.

'It's very dark, Mr Igor,' whispered Nanny.

'Beautifully so,' replied Igor, who wasn't in the least bothered about the dark. In fact, he much preferred it to horrible bright lights, sunshine and the like.

'I don't like the dark,' said Nanny. 'I wish I 'ad me torch.'

'You *do* have your torch, Nanny.'

'I know, but it doesn't seem to be throwin' out much light. I think the batteries needs changin'.'

'Try switching it on,' sighed Igor.

'Silly me!' said Nanny. 'That's better!'

The pair reached the door.

'We must be very quiet,' whispered Igor. 'Remember, we're only here to establish what those two dubious-looking characters are up to. Try not to attract milord's attention. We mustn't embarrass him.'

'I know, Mr Igor,' trilled Nanny. 'We've got to keep a low . . . er, what do they call it . . . a low profile, that's it!'

'Rather difficult for you, Nanny,' said Igor drily.

Nanny's massive bulk pushed against the door. 'Don't worry, Mr Igor. I'll be as quiet as a mouse . . .!'

Crash! The door was wrenched from its ancient hinges.

Duckula almost fell from the sofa in fright. At first, for a second or two, he imagined he was still in Castle

Duckula. He soon realised he wasn't . . . and the thought of his own, safe little bed was suddenly very inviting.

What *was* that terrible noise? Duckula didn't wait to find out. He crawled along the floor, around the sofa, and hid behind it. With a tremendous effort, he tried to stifle his heavy gasps of fear. But, try as he might, he could still hear his own breathing, and it seemed so strange: whir . . . whirr . . . whirr!

Wait! What was *this*? His hand rested on a machine of some sort, on the floor beside the sofa. A noisy tape-recorder – so that was the 'breathing' sound!

Duckula was so annoyed, he almost forgot to be scared! Who could have put it there? Probably Sandy Swift checking up, he thought. What a nerve these newspaper types have. They don't trust *anyone*. Well, he wasn't going to be spied on, he decided, and he turned it off.

Upstairs, the two professors made their way from one room to another.

'Where should we position the ultra-sensitive spectre detector?' mused Dafty. 'How about under this four-poster bed?'

'Ideal,' said Owlie. 'Now, how about our newly invented ghoul trap? Ah! There's a loose floorboard here, just by the bed! We can lay the trap there. Where's my torch?'

They gently lifted the carpet and found the floor-board. It was very loose. In fact, it was more like a trapdoor. Owlie shone his torch down and almost yelled in excitement, 'A secret staircase, Dafty!'

'So it is, old fellow! Might lead down to the cellars.

When I was researching the history of this place, I discovered that in the Middle Ages there were dungeons and torture chambers. Bound to be skeletons and such there. Just the place for restless spirits.'

'Shall we go down?'

Although both Dafty and Owlie were scared of ghosts, they were also intensely curious about them. Despite their fear, they simply had to follow the stairs. Dafty led the way . . . down . . . down . . . down . . . spiralling and twisting. It was dark and dusty, with centuries of cobwebs.

Then, to their horror and fascination, they heard a sound coming up the stairs, towards them; a lilting, hypnotic tune played on a violin! The stairs were so narrow and winding that they couldn't see who – or what – was responsible for it.

The terrified duo didn't wait to face this particular music! They turned and scrambled back up the stairs and through the trapdoor. They kept on running down the main staircase and then down another flight of stairs into the kitchens!

6

Nanny's Here!

The bats sat outside the Castle clock.

'Any idea where we are?' asked Sviatoslav.

'Search me,' replied his friend Dmitri. 'We're in the dark, as usual!'

'I heard the duck saying something about going to a haunted house . . .' said Sviatoslav.

'You mean to say these characters are *visiting* a haunted house? Don't you mean they're going to *haunt* it?!'

'Hee, hee! Ha, ha! Ho, ho!' The bats laughed so much, they nearly shook to the floor!

Now back to the professors, who were still puzzling over the strange violin music.

'Was it . . . could it possibly have been one of the phantom fiddlers?' asked the breathless Professor Barn-Owl.

'You mean as reported in *Famous Phantom Fiddlers* by Fred Fiddlesticks, the equally famous ghost-hunter? Mmm, yes, old chap, I think it was!' replied his colleague, flopping down on a chair and wiping his brow with an already grubby handkerchief, which was soon even grubbier! Both professors were covered from head to foot in dust and dirt.

It was darker down here, without the moon shining in. Luckily, they had kept hold of their torches, despite their panic in escaping from the mysterious musician on the secret staircase!

Owlie thought he heard something: like a dull thud or a very heavy footstep from the ground floor, just above them.

Dafty could hear it too, but he tried to stay calm. 'I'm sure it's not the phantom fiddler. Probably just a rat, I expect.'

Owlie thought it sounded more like an elephant than a rat. 'I suggest we find ourselves a good hiding place. Merely to keep watch on potential phenomena, you understand. Heaven knows, we're not cowards, are we, Dafty?'

'Of course we're not!' agreed his friend. 'We'll keep watch . . . from a safe place!'

The 'elephant', otherwise known as Nanny, was actually walking as softly as she could manage. 'I can't see Duckyboos anywhere,' she whispered to Igor. 'In fact, I can't see *anything* . . .'

'You've switched your torch off again, Nanny,' Igor pointed out.

'Ooh, so I 'ave!'

'Don't forget, Nanny, we don't want the master to notice us. We merely wish to locate the two strangers. Shall we go down these stairs? They probably lead to the kitchens. If I know Master Duckula, he'll be down there! But remember – absolute silence!'

'All right, Mr Igor. Ooh, I feel all of a tremble.'

'Well please try not to tremble, Nanny. You're making this suit of armour sha . . .' Igor's voice trailed off as the metal figure grabbed him from behind.

Nanny, oblivious to Igor's misfortune, started down

the stairs. 'C'mon Mr Igor,' she called. 'Don't be such a slowcoach!'

Duckula had climbed back on the sofa and was dreaming tasty dreams of broccoli sandwiches, steaming mugs of cocoa with chocolatey bits on top, jam doughnuts . . . and electronics sets!

He licked his beak, yawned, stretched out his legs a little and turned over, just as he did every night in his own bed. Only he wasn't in his own bed! He was on the sofa in the great hall of the haunted house and this time, when he turned over, he landed with a bump on the floor.

'Nanny!' he cried. 'I've fallen out of bed!'

It took just a few seconds for the horrible truth to sink in! He felt quite cross with himself. How silly of him to shout like that, as if he expected his beloved Nanny to come running to comfort him.

But then the most amazing thing happened – for his beloved Nanny *did* come running to him! She was halfway down the stairs when she heard his call and came running back. As you know, Nanny was never one to stop and think before taking action! Especially where her little Duckyboos was concerned!

'I'm 'ere!' she called, as she turned and hurried through the gloom, crashing into pieces of sturdy old oak furniture and smashing them as if they were made from matchsticks.

Duckula could hardly believe it! Was it really Nanny, or a poltergeist pretending to be her? No, he decided, Nanny was like nothing else on earth – or even *beyond* the planet!

'Where are you, Duckyboos?' she cried. 'I can't find the bed you've fell out of!'

'There's no bed here, Nanny,' answered Duckula.

'Ooh, thank goodness for that! If there's no bed to fall out of, then you couldn't 'ave fell out o' bed! If there *'ad* been a bed, you might 'ave fell out of it an' bumped your 'ead!'

Duckula was convinced! This was his Nanny all right! 'What are you doing here?' he demanded, picking himself off the floor. Although he was secretly delighted to see Nanny, he also felt angry about being followed like this. He had to be alone. That was the condition. If the newspaper found out about this, he wouldn't get the money – and he'd be made to look a fool too!

'You're not supposed to be *here*!' he snapped, rubbing his head, which had begun to hurt a little. In fact, there was a lump on it.

'You *'ave* bumped your 'ead!' cried Nanny. 'I was right all the time. ''Ow you managed to fall out o' bed without a bed, I don't know! Whatever will you get up to next? 'Ere, let me rub some butter on it. That'll do the trick! I've got some in me sling. It should be nicely melted!'

'Nanny! Please don't fuss!' yelled Duckula. 'Now tell me what you're doing here or leave at once! This very minute!'

'Well, young fella me lad . . . you'll change your tune when you 'ear what Mr Igor and me 'ave to tell you,' she replied.

Duckula nearly exploded. 'Igor's here as well?' he cried, although, to be perfectly honest, deep, deep down, he was pleased to hear this too. 'Well, where is he?'

Nanny peered around the moonlit room. 'W . . . ell, 'e *was* 'ere. We was goin' down them stairs. 'E said that's where the kitchens would be.'

'He must have gone down without you,' said Duckula.

'Funny, I thought 'e was behind me.' Nanny's voice rose to a screech. 'You don't think them spooks 'ave got 'im, d'you, Duckyboos?'

Duckula thought this was highly unlikely: the sight of Igor was probably enough to scare spooks away! And if Nanny thought Igor was behind her, then, knowing Nanny, the chances were that he was really in front of her!

'Nanny, please! Tell me why you and Igor followed me here,' he pleaded. 'It wasn't just to keep an eye on me, was it?'

Nanny then told Duckula about the two strangers. He laughed it off, but a cold shiver seemed to slide down his back and he was glad his pair of trusty servants had decided to keep him company after all.

'Let's go down to the kitchen and see Mr Igor,' said Nanny. 'I'll make us all a nice pot of tea. That's what we need!'

Duckula had to agree. A cup of hot tea would go down very well, he thought. Especially with one of Nanny's coconut cakes . . . and especially if it had an extra cherry on top!

Nanny set off in the general direction of the stairs. I say *general* direction, because that's how Nanny moves around. Trifling obstacles, such as tables,

40

chairs, cupboards – and particularly doors! – are simply there to be bumped into, knocked aside and stamped into smithereens. Not that she means to be destructive, you understand. She's far too kindly; it's just Nanny being *Nanny*!

'Oh, drat!' cried Duckula, as he gathered his things together to follow Nanny. 'I must have fallen on my electronic ghost-repeller. I'll have to set it up again. Hang on for me, Nanny. Nanny, wait for me!'

But Nanny was already halfway down the stairs, singing happily to herself. 'Come on, Duckyboos,' she trilled. 'Mr Igor, are you there? 'Ave you put the kettle on? I've found Duckyboos an' e's all right, 'cept for a bump on 'is 'ead when 'e fell out of a bed that wasn't there, the young rascal!'

'That's it!' beamed Duckula, resetting his ghost-repeller. He was very pleased with himself about this clever little contraption. It must work, he thought; after all, he hadn't been bothered by any ghosts so far. Then he remembered that he didn't believe in ghosts anyway. Oh, never mind! he told himself, checking that he had the camera and electronics set. As for the packet of sandwiches, there was no need for them now Nanny was here, he thought, throwing them down on the sofa.

Why didn't Nanny wait, he grumbled, as he made his way through the great hall. Then he saw a sight that froze him in his tracks! He blinked. Was it a trick of the moonlight – or was that a suit of armour walking towards him?

7

Got a Can Opener?

Duckula swallowed hard. This wasn't a trick of the light and it wasn't his imagination. Slowly, clumsily, the metal-clad figure moved closer, making a ghastly, clanging noise. Was it one of the legendary ghosts – the spirit of a long-gone knight who fought in those crusades that Igor recalled now and then? Duckula didn't stop to think a second longer. He turned to run . . . to hide. Only a muffled yet comfortingly familiar voice stopped him.

'Milord, don't be afraid.'

'Igor!!!' Duckula almost sank to the floor with relief. 'Is . . . is it really and truly you?' Duckula couldn't actually see Igor's face behind the visor, and this place was making him so nervous that he was beginning to think ghosts were everywhere.

'Indeed, it is I, milord. I apologise sincerely for my demeanour. It is most unseemly, I know.'

'But what on earth are you doing inside that ridiculous suit of armour?' asked Duckula, starting to chuckle loudly. 'You do look funny! Tee-hee! Ha, ha!' The chuckle became a real honest-to-goodness belly laugh.

'Milord, I assure you my predicament is no cause for amusement.'

'Mabye not for you, Igor, but it is for *me*!'

'*Will* you help me get out of the wretched thing?' asked Igor.

'OK!' bellowed Duckula, doubling up with laughter. 'I'll see if I've got a can opener with me! Say, can you hear music? Like a violin being played?'

Igor listened. 'Very faintly, milord.'

'It's stopped now,' said Duckula. 'Strange! Perhaps it's a musical spook . . . tee-hee-hee!'

Down in the kitchen, the two professors were recovering from their ordeal on the secret staircase.

'Listen!' hissed Dafty. 'That noise is getting closer.'

Owlie listened. 'It's coming down the stairs! And . . . and it's *singing*!'

'The singing spectre!' they cried in unison.

'As mentioned in *Songs of the Spook Hit Parade*, compiled by Gary Ghoulman,' added Owlie.

'We must hide!' gasped Dafty.

'Ooh, but it's our duty to capture it in the interests of research, old fellow,' replied the other. 'But we must hide to . . . to watch it!'

'I agree. Purely for research purposes, of course.'

'Naturally, dear friend. Make for that larder – quick!'

Huddled together in the tiny larder, each professor tried not to let the other see how scared he was.

'Sorry I'm shaking,' whispered Owlie. 'Rather chilly in here. It's designed to keep food cold and fresh, you know.'

'Don't mention it!' murmured his companion.

'Tra la la . . .' Nanny was still singing happily to herself as she entered the kitchen. 'Mister Igor,' she called. 'Where are you?'

'The footsteps are so *heavy*!' gasped Dafty. 'I

43

wonder if we're experiencing a haunting by an entire Roman legion. There was a Roman encampment on the site of this house, you know.'

'That's it!' whispered Owlie excitedly. 'That explains the strange vernacular: 'misterigor'. Latin, of course!'

Nanny was exasperated. Where had Igor and Duckula got to? She supposed that Igor was looking for dungeons but where was Duckula? 'Duckyboos, Nanny's makin' tea now, you little scallywag,' she yelled.

'Duckyboos . . . Scallywag! Famous Roman generals,' whispered Owlie.

'I didn't know the Romans made *tea*,' said Dafty.

'Amazing! We've stumbled on an important and hitherto unknown fact of history,' answered his friend. 'We must publish a scientific paper about it!'

Nanny decided to turn on the light. She was finding it very difficult to make tea otherwise. For a start, she hadn't been able to find the kettle.

'That's better!' she declared. Now, where were the tea, sugar, cups, saucers and other tea-making equipment? Then she noticed the larder. Nanny much preferred a nice old-fashioned larder to modern kitchen cupboards. Not so long ago, the Castle kitchen had been fitted out in the latest style – but Nanny dismantled the units in less time than it took to install them!

She opened the larder door to find the pair of ghost-hunters staring at her with terrified eyes shining out of their dirty faces.

'Help!!' she yelled! These two looked more like chimney sweeps than spooks!

44

'It . . . it's the fabled sixteen-stone singing spectre!' spluttered Owlie.

'We must take courage,' cried Dafty. 'And capture it for posterity!'

'You're not capturing me for your posh ferret!' yelled Nanny, pushing the two professors back into the larder. They pushed back: she pushed forward; and all three fell against the wall, which seemed to give way and turn round, rather like a swing door. They were all stuck! After a few minutes of frantic wriggling, the door moved and one by one they found themselves thrown into what appeared to be a dark passage.

Owlie tugged at the door which had closed behind them but it was impossible to open it. The passage was quite narrow; Nanny touched both sides. She stood there, breathless, her enormous bulk heaving up and down.

'See what you've done!' she complained. 'Tryin' to get me for your ferret. Ferrets . . . aren't they dogs? Me ol' uncle Sid used to keep ferrets. Oooh! What a nerve! Wantin' me for a dog's dinner. I'm not bein' a dinner for any dog! I don't care 'ow posh it is!'

The two exhausted spook-finders thought what a peculiar spook Nanny was.

'Strange specimen,' muttered Dafty.

'I'm afraid it is our misfortune to be landed with a particularly tiresome spook,' sighed Owlie.

'I'm not bein' called a specimen an' a spook by a pair o' chimney sweeps!' Nanny was getting very cross now. She stamped her foot – a gesture which sent shock waves down the passage.

45

'Y – you're not a spook?' asked Dafty.

"Course I'm not! I'm . . . I'm a respectable Nanny!'

'Well, *we're* not chimney sweeps!' declared Owlie.

Nanny thought for a moment. If they weren't chimney sweeps they might be spooks. And Nanny wasn't going to spend any more time being insulted – especially not by *spooks*. She ran off as fast as her massive legs would carry her!

At last, Igor had managed to get out of his armour.

'I think you looked better with the visor *on*!' laughed Duckula. Igor ignored this remark and went on to explain how he'd been abducted before he could follow Nanny down the stairs.

Duckula's eyes widened. This was exciting stuff! He was feeling quite a bit braver now. 'Was it a ghost?' he asked.

'I doubt it, milord,' replied Igor drily. 'The scoundrel was very much flesh and blood . . . blood I'd dearly love to gain access to, milord. A spell in the dungeons would teach him . . .'

'Igor! Stop that! Now, start again . . . who was it?'

'Manners . . .'

'Igor! Never mind about teaching him manners with a spell of torture and all that stuff. I just want to know who could possibly have wanted to capture you.'

'But I told you, milord. *Manners* – Lord Windup's unspeakable butler!'

'You're kidding! I know you don't think he's the world's best butler, Igor, but surely you don't imagine he's a kidnapper as well?'

Igor was quite certain. 'You're not suggesting I'm telling untruths, milord?'

'Er, no. I believe you. But how did he overpower you and make you . . . tee hee . . . dress up in that suit of armour?'

'He threatened to harm you, milord. I – I had to submit to the ignominy of climbing into that – that device to protect you!'

'Igor, you're a hero! But why would he want to harm *me*?'

'Things are amiss, sir.'

'If you mean there's some funny business going on, I agree. But what?'

'Who knows, milord?'

'Didn't he give you any clues?'

'Well, milord . . . there was something. I'm not sure it's significant, but Manners's manner of speech was different.'

'Manners's manner? Of speech? Igor, d'you mean he was talking in another voice to fool you? What was it like? Italian? German? Cockney? Transylvanian Lower Middle Class?'

'It rather reminded me of the way the characters speak in those . . . those horribly light-hearted programmes that Nanny is so fond of. *Soap operas*, I believe is the term commonly used.'

'Australian!' cried Duckula. 'So Manners is really an *Australian*!'

'It would seem so, milord.'

'Mmmm, we must get to the bottom of this, Igor!'

'Must we, milord?'

'Yes, Igor! Don't you see? We've stumbled on a mystery!'

8
Goosewing and Cork Hats!

High up in an attic of the west wing of Windup Hall, a makeshift laboratory had been set up. A funny little goose-like fellow was fussing around a very complicated piece of equipment. As he added a bit more solution to this test tube, adjusted that Bunsen burner and twiddled with numerous switches, he talked to himself.

This was none other than Doctor Von Goosewing, Duckula's avowed enemy. Actually, he wasn't exactly talking to himself, but to Heinrich, his friend. Heinrich wasn't real, however, but an imaginary companion invented by Von Goosewing because he didn't have any proper friends – probably because he spent all his time thinking of ways to exterminate vampires, especially Count Duckula!

'You see, Heinrich, vhen I am consulting mine long-range wampireometer, I am seeing zat zee dreaded wampire Count Dugula is in ziss haunted house, zo I am coming here. It's a great pity zat vhen I arrive, zee machine has developed a minor fault und cannot tell me zee exact position of zee fiend. It iss such a *big* house too! I am out of zee breath valking up und down zese stairs.

'Never mind, Heinrich! Vhen I locate zee monster, it vill all be worth zee effort! I haff almost perfected zee latest wersion of mine ultra-sophisticated

48

wampire-waporiser. It iss zee last vord in wampire-destroying technology. Soon Dugula vill be reduced to a puff of smoke!

'I am getting in a tizzy-vizzy wiz excitement! Vhen I put zee finishing touches to mine waporiser, it vill end zee Dugula dynasty, vhich has been zee curse of my life for zo long. Ziss machine is designed to overcome zee effects of your run-of-zee-mill ghosts – und zoom straight for zee evil being. You could say it iss a spooked-up model! Ach, *spooked-up*! Good joke, eh, Heinrich? I am a comedian as vell as a genius!'

'Let's go down to the kitchen,' said Duckula to Igor. 'Nanny should have made tea by now! Say, I'm getting to feel quite at home. I think I'll turn the lights on.'

'I would advise against it, milord. If you recall, part of the agreement you signed was that you faced the prospect of the supernatural in the dark. Speaking for myself, I much prefer the gloom.'

'Well, you would wouldn't you? and speaking for myself, I'd like the lights on!'

'But how about the media representatives in the caravans . . . and Lord and Lady Windup in the cottage? They'll notice.'

'Mmm, perhaps you're right,' replied Duckula. 'Though I've got my doubts about the Windups, after what you've just told me.'

'Milord, I'm sure a genuine English aristocrat wouldn't knowingly employ a ne'er-do-well as a butler,' answered Igor snootily. 'Butlering is a noble calling.'

'Oh, it is, is it?' mocked Duckula. 'Well, I'm not so

sure Lord Windup is any more noble than his sneaky butler. In fact, I wonder if he's a proper lord at all!'

'The seat is perfectly genuine, milord. I often read the society pages in the English newspapers and I've noticed the name mentioned quite often. Why, just the other day I read a newspaper report of Queen Victoria's Jubilee.'

'Igor!' snapped Duckula. 'You're *years* out of date! Just like those cheese biscuits Nanny gave us for tea last week . . . what did it say on the tin . . .? Oh yes, "as currently issued to serving soldiers in the Napoleonic Wars". What's more, Igor, you're an-out-of-date *snob*! And by the way, I didn't question whether the old boy's seat was genuine. I saw that for *myself* – he was sitting on it! I merely doubted whether *he* was genuine!' grinned Duckula, laughing at his little joke.

'Very *droll*, sir,' said Igor.

'I thought so! Tee-hee-hee! Now, all that talk of nonsense and biscuits has made me peckish. Let's find Nanny and get something to eat! Hey, I think I'll eat my sandwiches right now, just in case Nanny's not managed to rustle up anything tasty yet. I put them on that sofa . . . now, where are they? Lend me that spare torch, Igor.'

The sandwiches had gone, but the paper Nanny had wrapped them in was still there! Duckula picked it up. He knew it was his sandwich wrapping . . . how else would the front cover of the *Transylvanian Times*, complete with crumbs, have landed on a sofa in a haunted house?

'Igor! There must be some pretty hungry spooks here!' called Duckula. 'We're going to find Nanny and then the three of us are going to search this place from top to bottom!'

'That's what you think, me old mate! Ha! Ha! Ha!' The voice was gruff and mean.

Duckula swung round. The torch showed up a leering character with a haversack on his back and wearing a hat with corks swinging from it.

'Manners!' blurted Igor. 'You should be ashamed to call yourself a butler! You're a disgrace to the profession. How dare you wreak emotional blackmail upon me by threatening to harm my master, Count Duckula!'

'I'll wreak more than blackmail on you if you don't stop giving me lugholes a sting like a gnat's bite on a sheared sheep's back!'

'Milord, this is the vulgar specimen who humiliated me earlier.'

'It's *you* who'll be a specimen, sport . . . in a pickle jar!' roared the cork-hatted creature.

Duckula stared in astonishment. It was Manners, all right. At least, it looked like Manners. Exactly like him, in fact. But the clothes . . . the suntan . . . the voice, they were all so different. It was utterly puzzling.

'He deserves a spell in the dungeons, milord!' said Igor.

'You'll have a spell in the outback with an empty water bottle, me old mate!' grinned 'Manners'.

'I am not your "old mate",' snapped Igor. 'And nor am I a – a *sport*!

'He's right!' chuckled Duckula. 'Igor's no sport! Why, he can't even play a decent game of *tiddlywinks*!'

'A comic, eh?' 'Manners's' tone grew colder and he sneered at them in a dastardly, calculating way, as if he were wondering what to do with them.

Duckula shivered. Perhaps it would have been better just to *save up* for his electronics set, he thought.

'Puff . . . puff . . . pant . . . pant!' Nanny rushed down the narrow, winding passage. Where she was going, she didn't know. She had only two intentions: firstly, to get away from those two spooks who wanted to feed her to their dog and secondly, to get back to her precious Duckula. As she rushed on, the sound of a melodic tune, played on a violin, wafted through the cold, stale air. Funny, she thought. Then it stopped and she forgot about it.

The passage was lit by dim lights placed on either side of the wall at intervals, but it was very dirty; and, worst of all, in places Nanny could hardly squeeze through it! She could hear the sound of the fearsome pair close behind her, but she dared not look back. It would have been *impossible* for her to look back, because there was no room for her to turn round!

Actually, the two ghost-hunting professors would have preferred to pass her, but that wouldn't have been an easy task!

'I suppose it's rather exciting, finding a real secret passage!' gasped Dafty.

'I daresay,' breathed Owlie, but I do wish we could overtake this . . . this . . . whatever it is!'

'Mmm, I must say, it does seem very robust for a spectre,' panted his colleague.

'Look!' cried the other. 'There's a ladder ahead. The way out!'

Nanny reached the rope ladder first. It was very narrow and very steep. With a desperate effort, she climbed up while the two professors scrambled behind her. She reached a door and flung herself at it. Like a huge, beached whale, she dragged herself through the open doorway, then realised that her two pursuers were only a couple of metres away. But the ancient rope wouldn't hold any more, and the learned ghost-hunters – each holding a piece of torn rope – were forced to leap back to the cold stone floor of the passage.

'I thought I'd never escape those spooks,' gasped Nanny, glancing around her new surroundings. 'Ooh, I'm in the library. Wonder if they've got any nice storybooks?'

'Er, guten Morgen, madam!'

Poor Nanny leapt in shock at the sudden voice. Not *another* spook, surely?

A Strange Encounter

It was Doctor Von Goosewing, of course! He had finished his marvellous machine and was wandering around the house in search of Duckula. Unfortunately, the contraption was quite heavy for a goose of his size to carry around, so he'd put it on the lower tray of a tea-trolley from the dining room.

He wheeled the trolley into the spacious library. This might be a good spot, he thought. But then he had slight doubts. Zee wampire doesn't do much reading of serious literature, he told himself. He reads only silly comics. Zee monster is uneducated – unlike *me*!

Von Goosewing was standing in the library, talking to himself, when to his amazement a section of the book-lined wall opened up and in burst the biggest hen he'd ever seen, puffing and panting and absolutely covered in cobwebs.

'You seem to be in some distress, mine dear!' he said.

'Distress?' cried the breathless Nanny. 'Isn't that a kind of indigestion?'

'Er, it *could* be,' answered Von Goosewing. What a strange creature this was!

'I've been chased down a dark passage by two spooks,' blurted Nanny.

Von Goosewing peered closely at the hen. He had a funny feeling he'd seen her before. 'Oh, vhat an ordeal for you,' he sympathised.

Nanny collapsed on an antique chair with bowed legs, which immediately became even more bowed under her weight.

Suddenly, she remembered her fear. 'You're not a ghost, are you?' He didn't seem like a ghost . . . in fact, he seemed strangely familiar to her.

'No, no, no! I am a doctor!'

'Ooh, a doctor!' Nanny was greatly relieved. 'Can you take a look at me left big toe, then? It's been givin' me a bit o' trouble lately . . .'

'Er, later . . . later. I'm busy just now. Tell me, vhat are you doing here in zee haunted house. *You're* not a ghost, are you?'

'Ooh, dear me, no!' said Nanny.

'Vell, are you maybe a servant?'

'Yes . . . I suppose I am.'

'You vork for Lord Vindup?'

'No, 'course not,' laughed Nanny. 'I work for count Duckula . . . I'm his Nanny.'

'*Count Dugula?*' Goosewing trembled. So this harmless hen was not so harmless after all!

'And "work" is *the* word for it, *I* can tell you,' continued Nanny. 'The young rascal 'as me runnin' up and down them Castle stairs with cups o' cocoa an' jam doughnuts all day long. No wonder me big toe's – '

'Vhere *is* your master?' spluttered Goosewing, stepping back from Nanny. He was shaking with the impact of what he'd just heard.

'That's what I'd like to know,' replied Nanny. 'I thought 'e was behind me, but 'e wasn't. Never mind. 'E'll come runnin' when 'e 'ears me shouting . . .

'specially as I've got some lovely chocolate wafers in me sling!'

Von Goosewing's mind was racing. He decided on a plan of deception. With a bit of luck, this repulsive creature might lead him to the dreaded fiend. Then, he thought, she too will perish with the vampire Dugula!

Now all this time, Duckula and Igor were still in the great hall with the cork-hatted 'Manners', who had become nastier and nastier. The pair were obviously a gret nuisance to him.

'Excuse me,' said Igor icily. 'But may we go down into the kitchens?'

'No, you may not, and shut yer trap while I think!' replied 'Manners'.

'But Nanny's waiting for us,' Duckula explained.

Their captor's cruel eyes brightened, as a devious ploy to keep the two under control occurred to him.

'Nanny? You mean that sheila who's the size of a double-decker bus?'

'An accurate description, but most unacceptable from one of your ilk,' said Igor.

'You won't find her!' grinned the magpie. 'I've got her safely out of harm's way!'

'You've *captured* Nanny?' Duckula was horrified.

'Good and proper!' lied the creature, the corks on his hat swinging triumphantly. 'Tied her up! Took a couple o' miles o' rope, mind yer! Now she's somewhere you won't find her in a hurry!'

'An outrage!' Igor bristled with anger.

'And what's more,' continued their tormentor, 'if

you two swagbellied sheepdips don't do exactly as you're told – which is to stay right where you are – then I'll take the outsized witch and throw her in the duckpond to see if she sinks or swims! Understand?'

Duckula and Igor nodded. They understood all right! Poor Nanny was in the evil clutches of this . . . whoever he was; a question over which Duckula was still puzzling. 'Are . . . are you Manners, Lord Wind-up's butler?' he asked timidly.

The magpie merely laughed and retorted, 'Manners? You mind *your* manners, asking nosy questions! Ask any more an' I'll clip yer beak! Now, both sit down on that sofa and watch this!'

He then took something from his large canvas bag. A kind of stick. When the moonlight caught the object, Duckula could see that it was a boomerang and, in spite of feeling terrified, humiliated and very cross, he couldn't help but be a teeny bit fascinated. It was the very first time he'd seen a real boomerang!

'Watch!' commanded 'Manners', as he took expert aim. Whizzzz! went the boomerang right to the far end of the large hall. Duckula and Igor turned their heads to follow its progress as it skimmed through the air.

Moonlight was streaming in through the big windows, and Duckula's eyes had become used to the dim light anyway. So he saw clearly how, as it passed the big fireplace, the thin, tapered end of the boomerang caught the handle of a small china flower basket, wrenched it from the mantelpiece, and carried it back to the grinning magpie, who promptly put it in his pocket!

Duckula and Igor were astounded: stealing by boomerang!

'Clever, eh?' said 'Manners'. 'No one else in the world can do that! I taught myself to do it when I spent twenty years all by myself, lost in the outback! I have my boomerangs specially made now!'

'A cheap trick!' was Igor's comment.

'No cheap remarks from you, old vinegar face!' said their leering captor, taking something from his other pocket and beginning to eat.

'My sandwiches!' cried Duckula.

'Mmmm, not bad!' grunted the magpie, his mouth full.

'You *stole* them!' said Duckula.

''Course I stole 'em! I steal anything and everything, so shut up while I eat – or *else*!' And the greedy creature sat down in an armchair and put his grubby feet up on a polished table. Every few minutes he took a swig of water from a bottle.

Duckula and Igor felt so helpless. What could they do to help Nanny? Come to think of it, what could they do to help *themselves*?

10

Too Many Questions!

Von Goosewing and Nanny were making slow progress, trudging through the house. What with the
doctor pushing the tea-trolley and Nanny complaining
about her sore toe, it wasn't an easy journey. Luckily,
being the shortest night, daylight was just beginning
to break through, though the wind was still howling
outside. In other words, it was a typical English
Midsummer's night!

'Duckyboos! Duckyboos!' called Nanny every now
and then. This made Von Goosewing break out in
goosepimples. To be so close to ridding the world of
Duckula was almost too much! Indeed, even being so
close to the vampire's Nanny was traumatic for the
doctor and he tried to keep his distance. Who knows
what evil brews in the tiny brain of the huge hen, he
thought. Mind you, it wasn't easy to keep your
distance when walking next to Nanny!

'That's a funny machine you've got there, Doctor,'
Nanny commented. 'I suppose it's very clever and
gets rid of 'orrible germs and things. I've got a tin of
ointment in me sling that does wonders for knees.
Trouble is, me knee's all right . . . it's just me big toe
that's not. Could your machine do anything for me?'

'Oh . . . sorry, mine dear! You are right, though. It
iss a very clever machine – but not for *toes*!' smiled
Von Goosewing slyly.

'You must 'ave to be clever to be a doctor,' said Nanny.

Much as he despised and feared Nanny, Von Goosewing couldn't help but feel flattered. 'Ja, I am a genius in fact! I am talented in all fields.'

'Ooh, you're a *farmer* as well?'

'Nein, nein! I mean I am a genius at physics, mathematics, chemistry, microbiology, astronomy, aerodynamics, wood-carving, paper plane-making, sink-unblocking, music – '

'Music! I bet you play the violin!' cried Nanny.

'Ja! I like to play Mozart.'

'No, the violin – not the mozart.'

'Ja! I play Mozart on zee wiolin!' So stupid! Perhaps she doesn't have a brain at all, thought Von Goosewing. Maybe Dugula had removed it!

'Oooh, I see,' said Nanny. 'Well, I'm glad we've got to the bottom of that mystery!'

More puzzled than ever, Von Goosewing decided not to pursue the conversation any further.

Back in the great hall, Duckula and Igor were still being guarded by their shifty-eyed guard, who had made their ordeal even worse by singing and humming tuneless songs in a terrible voice. It was obvious that the more painful this was to his captive audience, the more he was enjoying himself! Duckula and Igor were used to listening to silly songs badly sung – they lived with Nanny, after all – but *this* was even more agonising!

Something occurred to Duckula. 'Do you play any musical instruments? The violin, for example?'

60

'Yeah, I've played a mean fiddle in me time . . . mostly round a campfire during a good old sing-song! Helped to keep the dingos at bay!'

Duckula thought that this character's singing would keep anything at bay, but he didn't say so! Instead, he asked, 'But do you play the violin these days?'

'Too many questions, sport!' snapped the magpie. 'Stop asking me dumb things, you nosy little waddler! It's none of your business what I do! Just watch your manners! Hee! Hee!'

Manners is watching *us*, not the other way round, thought Duckula. That's if he *was* Manners. The sorry little Count felt so helpless. They must think of some way to escape, and quickly! It was lighter now, and Duckula took the opportunity to take a good look at their rude companion. He was so like Lord Wind-up's butler – and yet he *wasn't*! Who was he really? What was going on in this rambling mansion? What a mystery!

Duckula peered at his captor with intense curiosity, and the more he peered, the more confused he became. If this really was Manners, how could he be so different so soon? He must be a master of disguise!

Footsteps were approaching the great hall. Duckula and Igor sat up on their prison sofa and listened. Was it Nanny? It didn't sound like Nanny!

'Don't get excited, you pair of feather-brained bookends! It's probably Good-Time Charlie!' declared 'Manners'.

Duckula leapt up in surprise. So Charlie was involved as well!

'Manners' greeted Charlie with a hearty slap on the back.

'Sorry I've been so long,' beamed the newcomer. 'I lost track of the time.'

'Well, me old mate, did yer find anything?' asked the other.

'Not yet,' answered Charlie. 'But it must be in the library. I could have tapped more walls and maybe found the entrance to the passage, given more time.'

'You and your time!' growled Manners. 'I don't have unlimited time, you clock-faced fool!'

'Oh, I say!' Charlie looked very deflated. 'Have I got time to show you what progress I've made?'

'OK. But it'd better be worth my time, sport, or your time'll be up!'

The cork-hatted creature roared with laughter at his own joke and then, his mood swiftly turning grim, he turned to Duckula and Igor and snarled; 'Stay right there, you two. Remember what'll happen to your Nanny if you don't! Say, what's this?' he added, picking up the tape-recorder. 'Planning to trick us into opening our mouths too much?'

'No. It's not mine, honestly!' answered Duckula.

The evil guard grinned and turned on the machine. 'It'll come in handy if you two decide to plan anything! See yer later! C'mon, Charlie, let's go.'

'Glad they've gone,' whispered Duckula, bending down and turning off the tape-recorder.

Igor thought this seemed a very reckless gesture. 'Is that wise, milord?'

'We can turn it back on in a few minutes, but we've got to talk,' explained Duckula.

'Milord, I'm loathe to say this,' replied Igor, 'but you do seem to have landed us in an unenviable position. This ruthless creature has insulted the noble House of Duckula and must be punished with the utmost severity. I've marked him down for a prolonged spell on the new torture rack in the Castle dungeons. The implement is hardly three centuries old and needs just slight lubrication with a can of oil and it'll be in perfect working order!'

'Igor, if we don't sort out what's going on in this place, we'll be lucky if we ever get back to the Castle. We've got to do something now! What did Charlie say about a passage . . .?'

'Sir, the villain has made threats against Nanny, and despite our differences I don't wish to see her harmed by that . . . that foul rogue!'

Duckula was angry, too. Being made to sit on a sofa and take cheeky comments from a magpie wearing a hat with corks on it was humiliating. 'D'you think he is Lord Windup's butler?' he asked Igor.

'If he is, then he's certainly undergone a radical transformation,' was Igor's comment. 'I wonder, milord . . . I wonder . . .'

'Spit it out, Igor. What do you wonder?'

'Milord, I don't wish to alarm you, but such a metamorphosis is not a natural phenomenon in ordinary mortals. It occurs to me that this creature could possibly be a supernatural being of a very low order. Infinitely lower down the scale than the venerable vampires, such as yourself, and lower even than mischievous ghosts and goblins. I did warn you, milord, that old houses can harbour grossly uncouth

63

and primitive beings whose personalities are hardly formed and absolutely unversed in the exquisitely refined tortures and cruelties of the higher orders – such as *you* should be, if things had turned out as they should have!'

Duckula waited for Igor to finish. 'Igor! Were you trying to tell me, in your usually extremely boring way, that you think old Aussie swagface is really a spook?'

'Er, that about sums it up, milord.'

Duckula slapped his thigh in an imitation of Manners – a gesture he rather admired. 'Ouch! That hurt!' he murmured. 'Anyway, kangaroos' feet and crocodiles' teeth!' Duckula had been trying to think up explosive expressions to match those of Manners and he was quite pleased with these efforts!

'I beg your pardon, Master Duckula?' asked Igor, coldly. Having his carefully considered theory scorned had clearly hurt his feelings!

'That just about sums up what I think of your long-winded theory, Igor! Because I've got a much better theory of my own!'

11
Double Trouble!

Igor surveyed Duckula with disdain. The young master was enjoying all this far too much!

'And what's your theory then, milord?'

'Look-alikes!'

'You mean twins?'

'They could be twins, but I don't think so. Look at that,' said Duckula, pointing to their captor's canvas bag, which was lying on the floor. 'See the initials?' On the side of the bag were the letters E. E. 'If he were Mitch Manners, he'd have M. M. on his bag!'

'Most perceptive, milord.'

'Yes! It makes *sense*! Nanny was watching a soppy old movie one wet afternoon last week and it was all about two people who looked alike. Now, *how* did the plot go . . . I was only half watching it, 'cos I was playing with . . . I mean working on . . . my electronics set.'

'I urge caution against being too influenced by Nanny's taste in films,' said Igor.

'But it all adds up, doesn't it, Igor? The two look-alikes have hatched a wicked plot!'

'What plot, may I ask?'

'I don't know, Igor! But we'll find out, won't we?'

'If you say so, milord,' answered an extremely weary Igor. 'One other small point: it may not be his bag. Probably stolen property!'

Duckula grimaced. Why did Igor always have to pour cold water on his best ideas?

'Another thing . . .'

'Yes, Igor?'

'We'd better turn the tape-recorder back on, before E. E. or M. M. returns.'

And why did he always think of everything, mused Duckula, who'd been so carried away he'd forgotten about that!

The thin, watery rays of early morning sunlight filtered through the windows of Windup Manor, although it was still several hours before morning proper . . . and even longer before dawn, Eastern Transylvanian time, when Castle Duckula would automatically return to its mountaintop home.

The two ghost-hunters, Dafty and Owlie, however, were still very much in the dark!

'I'm beginning to think we'll never find our way out of this maze of secret passages,' groaned Dafty.

'Never give up hope, my dear friend,' replied Owlie. 'Now, if we could discover where we took a wrong turning, we might find our way back to the kitchen larder.'

'But we seem to be going round in circles,' said his companion. 'That "Nanny" thing . . . real or ghostly, I don't care any more . . . has certainly caused us a great deal of trouble.'

'Perhaps the creature was real,' remarked Owlie, bitterly. 'No apparition, ghost, spook, witch or spectre, however malicious or mischievous, could possibly be such a nuisance!'

'Or weigh so much!' smiled Dafty; and if they hadn't both felt so miserable, they would have laughed.

On and on they walked, this way and that, chalking signs on the walls every now and then, so they'd know if they wandered back to the same spots; clever professors always carry pieces of chalk with them! But they kept coming back to the same places. It was simply impossible to know which way to go in the rabbit warren of dark, dank passages which sometimes opened out into caverns and sometimes led up and down steps . . . but in the end, always seemed to lead nowhere.

'We're totally lost,' said Dafty. 'I doubt it we'll ever get out or if anyone will ever find us!'

'There's the music again,' said Owlie fearfully.

Dafty listened. The faint strains of the violin could be heard, as if from far, far in the distance.

'I've just had a brilliant idea!' Duckula suddenly told Igor as they sat on the sofa, just as they'd been ordered to.

'Really, sir?' Igor didn't seem at all interested.

'Yes! We don't need my ghost-repeller because, just as I thought, there are no ghosts here . . . just very real villains! So I'm going to transform it so it'll warn us if anyone real is following us. That way, we'll be able to search the house for clues!'

'Clues?'

'Yes, *clues*, Igor! To what's going on in this house!' replied Duckula, fiddling about with the wires and batteries. 'I'll put that one there, and join this one up with that . . . yes, that should do it!'

'One small detail, milord. We can't leave this room without endangering Nanny.'

'I know, Igor! But when we *do* leave this room, my device will make sure we won't be followed. In any case, Igor, this isn't just *any* room, it's the great hall. Look, there's a minstrels' gallery up there, which gives me another idea!'

'Oh . . . no!' Igor held his head in anguish.

'Yes, Igor. We can climb up there and escape!'

'But how about Nanny?'

'We can *find* Nanny! She can't be far . . . can she?'

'Who knows, milord. One thing I do know is that we are in danger from this creature, ghost or not. And he has an accomplice, don't forget.'

'You mean Charlie?' Duckula was surprised at Charlie. He seemed so nice. But what were they supposed to do . . . just sit around on a sofa? And then what? He might throw them all in the duckpond!

'I feel your idea is fraught with danger, sir, but I'm with you all the way, as they say in those films Nanny watches,' said Igor.

Duckula was encouraged by this rare example of an attempt at light-hearted humour by Igor. He knew that his faithful butler was really very nervous for their safety. And Duckula didn't feel all that brave himself!

The problem was how to climb up to the gallery before anyone returned. Duckula felt frightened and excited at the same time. He just hoped they weren't putting Nanny in danger.

'*You* climb up first,' he told Igor. 'You're taller than me. Then, once you're in the gallery you can pull *me* up.'

'We must move swiftly, milord. It would be very bad for you if the wretch returned to find me gone and you still here.'

The thought was horrible. 'Let's get on with it,' said Duckula, going cold with fear.

Igor climbed on a chair and then on to a tall dresser. From there it wasn't too difficult for him to clamber over the balcony into the gallery.

It was Duckula's turn. Putting his electronic warning device in his pocket, he followed the same steps as Igor had: on the chair, then the dresser. But, as he was shorter, he needed Igor to lean over and, with a hefty pull, heave him into the gallery.

'We made it!' gasped Duckula, joyfully.

'I'm unaccustomed to such activity!' remarked Igor. 'Most undignified!'

'Someone's coming into the hall,' hissed Duckula.

Kneeling down, the pair peeped over the balcony as the door to the great hall opened. Duckula was breathing so fast he felt sure his gasps would be heard downstairs!

'Manners' entered the great hall. 'Well, I'll climb a billabong!' he yelled! 'The yellow-beaked duck wasn't so yellow after all! He's got away . . . and so has his sour-faced servant! I didn't think they had the nerve . . . seemed like a pair of jelly trifles to me!' Then, with a loud, coarse belly laugh, he added, 'Well, they know what I told 'em . . . an' I meant what I said!'

'There's someone with him, milord,' whispered Igor. 'It's not Good-Time Charlie, is it?'

Duckula tried hard to see who the other was. And what he saw almost made him shout out loud.

'I was right! Look, Igor – another one! The look-alike!'

12
School Fiends!

It was true! Side by side they stood, Manners – Lord Windup's butler; and Manners – or E. E. – from Australia.

'You were right! There *are* two of them,' whispered Igor. 'I didn't doubt it, of course.'

'Oh, of course not, Igor,' grinned Duckula, almost leaping up and down, he was so delighted with his clever bit of detective work. 'Brilliant deduction, eh?'

'Brilliant, sir! Twins . . . or, according to your theory, they're doppelgangers.'

'No, they're magpies, Igor!' chuckled Duckula.

'Doppelgangers are look-alikes, milord. They say everyone has a double.'

'I hope you and Nanny don't have doubles,' giggled Duckula.

'We must keep our voices down, sir. The two are no doubt planning some mischief at this very moment. Let's listen.'

The cork-hatted one flopped down on the sofa and rested his feet on a small table, while the butler, walked over to the dresser, directly under where Duckula and Igor were hiding. For a terrible moment, Duckula imagined that the butler was going to climb up on to the dresser and then over the balcony.

Instead, he brought a large jug of what looked like lemonade and two glasses from the dresser and took them over to his double.

71

Duckula licked his lips at the sight of this. What he wouldn't give for a glass of lemonade and a cake with a big cherry on top! It seemed years since he'd eaten.

The doubles' voices carried in the still, early morning quiet of the not-so-very-empty house.

'Don't worry about *that* pair, Ed,' said the butler. 'we'll catch up with em'!'

'I'm gonna keep me promise,' laughed the other. 'I'll enjoy throwin' the old hen in the duckpond! She'll empty it, just like in that theory our old teacher used to try an' drum into us. You know the one, Bill, where you shout "Eureka"! Was it Pyphagersomebody's theory?'

'I know which one you mean. We'll have to shout "Eureka!" when we throw her in! And then again when we throw the snivelling little duck an' his stuffed shirt of a butler in!'

'Archimedes' Law,' whispered Duckula. 'What dunces they are!'

Actually, it was only by a great coincidence that Duckula had heard of this famous theory. A few days earlier, while waiting for a Transylvanian *Open Polytechnic* broadcast on electronics to begin, he'd had to sit through a few minutes of some boring mathematician rambling on about old Archimedes sitting in his bath and discovering his theory. To tell the truth, Duckula had found the story quite interesting, which is probably why the name had stuck in his head. Not that it would be there for much longer! Ask him about Archimedes next week and his head will be full of other things!

'The standard of modern education is disgusting,'

was Igor's whispered comment. 'Now, in my day, if you didn't know your tables forwards, backwards and sideways, a sharp swish of the cane was forthcoming. That's what errant pupils need.'

'All right, Igor. All right,' said Duckula, feeling grateful that he hadn't attended the same school as Igor. In fact, being a noble vampire Count, he hadn't attended *any* school. Remarkable how I've turned out so clever, he thought. A self-educated Count who could even recite Archimedes' Law. Well, OK – had a bit of an idea of Archimedes' Law!

The one who was evidently called Ed said, 'We never did so well at school, did we, Mitch? Drove our teachers crazy, our being so much alike in looks and in ways! We couldn't have been more like each other if we'd been real twins! And we still kept in touch with each other even after I went to live down under! We've done all right, eh? On the verge of being very, very rich! Think I'll retire with my share . . . buy me a nice big house . . . hey, think I might even have servants of my own!'

'Good idea! I'd like a butler of my own, after workin' as one for old Windup! My butler will have to be a better one than *I* was! I'll keep him on his toes! His Lordship had to put up with me – he was glad to get anyone to work in this house, with it being so haunted an' all!' Mitch's mocking laughter echoed round the hall.

'What would our old dads say if they could see us now?' sniggered Ed. 'Last time I went to see mine in jail . . . you know, when he was doing that long stretch for forging banknotes, I told him we'd be rolling in money one day!'

'They were school friends,' hissed Duckula. 'So Ed's not a *real* Australian. He went to live there a long time ago, and now, for some no-good reason, he's come back.'

'School *fiends* would be a more apt expression, milord.'

Mitch looked up. 'I heard a noise. Could be that duck and his ugly servant . . .!'

'Or something more intelligent,' suggested Ed. 'Like a rat!' And the pair roared with wicked laughter.

'How insolent!' Igor's face was twisting with annoyance at the irreverent tone.

It was time for Duckula and Igor to move on before they were found out. They crept low along the length of the gallery till they reached the door at the end. There were lots of potted plants in their way, so great care had to be taken not to knock any over or rustle any leaves. Opening the door was risky. Suppose it creaked? Suppose it was locked? Still bending low, Igor reached up and turned the doorknob. Very carefully and slowly, he pushed the door open just wide enough for them both to slip through.

This brought them into a corridor with bedrooms and bathrooms leading off it. Duckula was tempted to snuggle down in one of the beds, he was so exhausted, but Igor advised against it.

'You're right, Igor,' yawned Duckula. 'We've got to solve this mystery – and we've got to find Nanny quickly. First, there's something I've got to do.'

He took his electronic warning system from his pocket and proceeded to set it up.

'Look, Igor, here's how it works,' he said. 'I just turn it on, then place it three or four metres behind us. Then, if anyone – or anything – creeps along behind us, it lets out a high-pitched sound. Like this . . .'

'No, milord. Please don't test it yet. They'll hear.'

'You're right! Tee-hee! My enthusiasm for electronic wizardry is going to my head. Anyway, I place the warning system three or four metres behind us . . .'

'Why three or four metres, milord?'

'What? Oh . . .'cos that's what it says in the instruction leaflet. Now, where was I?'

'Three or four metres behind yourself, milord,' sighed Igor.

'Oh yes. Well that's it, really.'

'But won't we need a tape measure?' asked Igor.

'What for?'

'To measure three or four metres, milord.'

Duckula glanced at Igor's face. It was as deadpan as ever. Sometimes he couldn't be sure whether his butler was making fun of him. 'It's only *approximate*, Igor. Approximately three or four metres.'

'I see. But one other thing . . .'

'What's that, Igor?'

'Whenever you run back to move the . . . the device along, won't your close proximity set the sound off?'

'Ah! Ah! I can tell you have no idea about electronics, Igor. See this?' Duckula held out a small metal box. 'This is the remote control box. Before I return to the system, I immobilise it with this!'

'Most ingenious, sir,' said Igor, the faintest of smiles curling his thin lips.

'Now, let's get going,' said a flustered Duckula. 'We're wasting time.'

'*Time*? Do'you have the time?' came a sudden voice from behind them.

13
Off Your Trolley!

Duckula and Igor were shocked to see Good-Time Charlie.

'How you have the audacity to ask us the time is beyond me!' exploded Igor.

'Oh, is it beyond you? I'm surprised!' replied Charlie with a big smile. 'Can't tell the time at your age! I must say you're up early, aren't you? It's not really getting-up time yet, you know. Mitch has asked me to look for someone who's out to make trouble . . . the big fat hen. Have you seen her, or haven't you had time?'

'This is insufferable!' cried Igor. 'Allow me to incarcerate the wretch!'

'I say,' said Charlie, 'this is no time to talk like that!'

'Oh, yes it is!' said Duckula. 'C'mon, Igor, let's incarcerate him, or why don't we just lock him in that big linen basket over there?'

'Good idea, milord.'

'But you don't understand,' spluttered Charlie. 'Give me time to explain . . .'

'You're working for Mitch and Ed, aren't you?' asked Duckula.

'Yes, but . . .'

'And if you catch Nanny, the – er – big fat hen you mentioned, they're going to throw her in the duckpond?'

77

'Yes, but . . .'

'Well, for your information, that hen may be big and fat, but she's my Nanny and she's not going in any duckpond for you or anyone else! Into the basket . . .'

'Perhaps we might extract some information from him first, milord,' suggested Igor.

'I can't tell you anything!' cried Charlie. 'I have to keep the plans secret all the time! My loyalty is to Mitch and Ed. They've taught me all I know!'

'They couldn't teach you good manners!' grinned Duckula. 'That's something they know nothing about!'

'Quite so!' exclaimed Igor.

'I've a good mind to teach him a lesson with my electronics set!' said Duckula.

Charlie grimaced. That sounded painful! He decided it was time he gave up and volunteered to go in the linen basket! It looked fairly comfortable and airy, because it was made of wicker and full of holes. 'Actually, when I think about it, being shut in the basket will give me a good excuse to get out of capturing the big fat . . . I mean, your Nanny. She *is* a bit too much for me to handle!' he confessed.

'Nanny's too much for *anyone* to handle,' laughed Duckula.

So, with Charlie safely and quite comfortably in the big roomy basket, Duckula and Igor carried on in their search for clues and Nanny.

How surprised Duckula would have been if he could have seen Nanny at that moment – wandering around with his old enemy, Doctor Von Goosewing!

They hadn't really got very far. It wasn't easy pushing a tea-trolley through the rambling house: up and down stairs, along corridors, in and out of rooms and generally all over the place in an aimless fashion.

'Ziss is a very confusing house,' grumbled Von Goosewing. 'Vhat a pity my wampireometer iss out of action.'

'What does that do?' asked Nanny, breathless.

'Vhy, it iss just zee zing to find your Master, Count Dugula.'

'Oh, that would be 'andy! I'm very worried about Duckyboos. I 'opes those two 'orrible chimney sweep spooks 'aven't got 'im.'

'Vot are you talking about? Chimney sveeps? I am surprised at zee wampire employing you. In all my life, never am I meeting a servant as incompetent.'

Nanny was delighted! What a lovely compliment, she thought. This funny little doctor was quite nice . . . although he did get a bit bad-tempered when she jolted his machine.

They reached a short, narrow flight of steps, leading down to a conservatory full of Lady Windup's plants. Duckula and Igor had passed through the conservatory just a few minutes earlier, but Nanny and Von Goosewing didn't know this, of course.

'Clang! Clang!' went the tea-trolley down the steps. Nanny was pushing it and Von Goosewing was in front, pulling.

'Take care, you silly ninny!' called the doctor in exasperation. 'Mine machine iss priceless. It iss not tea und plates of bread und butter you are pushing.'

'Oh, don't fuss, doctor. You're worse than Ducky-boos when I stand on his jigsaw puzzles!'

'For vot are you talking about puzzles? How can a hen be so stupid, zat iss vot puzzles me!'

'Now, Doctor, that's not nice. I 'opes you don't talk to your patients like that. I likes a doctor to 'ave a good bedside manner!'

'Shut up, if you please und manoeuvre my waporiser down zees steps . . . gently, gently. Svizzlesticks! You 'ave got it stuck!'

'Dear me, Doctor, so I 'ave,' trilled Nanny. *'I'm stuck, too!'*

The trouble was that Nanny had squeezed herself down between the wall and the trolley, in an effort to help matters.

'Don't worry, Doctor,' she said. 'I'll get meself free in a minute.'

But Nanny was well and truly fast against the wall. Neither she nor the trolley would budge!

'I'll climb over it,' said Nanny, lifting her enormous bulk onto the top layer of the trolley.

Von Goosewing was perched on the steps in front of the trolley, babbling helplessly. 'Be careful wid your big feet . . . do not be kicking my machine. Vot a clumsy creature you are! It iss on a diet you should be going, though vhen I've finished wiz you, there vill be no need for zat anyvay. Those sticky jam doughnuts zat you have up your arm vill be of no use to you . . .'

'It's all right, Doctor. I know what I'm doing! I've just got to get over the top of the trolley . . . help, it's moving!!'

Once Nanny had moved away from the side of the wall, the trolley had become dislodged, and when she heaved herself on top of the trolley, off it went! Clang! Crash! The trolley was hurtling down the steps with Nanny sprawled out on top like a huge teapot!

Down it went, knocking Von Goosewing out of the way, and then continued to the bottom of the steps, and down the slight incline towards the conservatory.

A battered and bruised Von Goosewing picked himself up. Waving his fist, he jumped up and down, hurting and aching all over.

'You flattened me! You are one stupid hen!' But his main concern was for his precious vampire-vaporiser. 'My machine vill be irrevocably damaged. It vill be out of commission . . . vhich iss exactly vhere you und your evil Master Dugula vill be ven I've finished wiz you.' He rubbed his chin thoughtfully. 'Eh, vait a minute, if my equipment iss broken, how vill I deal viz zee wampire? Oh, it iss too much! It iss a quick repair job I vill have to be doing.'

'Crash!' went the conservatory doors as the Nanny-driven tea-trolley burst through, scattering hundreds of plants and shuddering to an abrupt halt.

'Screeeech!!' The sound was ear-splitting. Yes, it was Duckula's electronic warning system in action! And what an astonishing and immediate effect it had on the plants! They began to grow and grow and grow till they'd engulfed Nanny and the trolley!

Within minutes, Nanny was completely covered in greenery! She had flowers in her hair, tickly ferns up her nose and sticking out of her ears and, worst of all, huge sticky leaves clinging all over her.

It was like a dense, damp, green jungle and Nanny was trapped in it. ''Elp! 'elp!' she cried, but her cries couldn't be heard by Duckula and Igor, who timidly crept back to see what had set the warning alarm off.

'Wow!' cried Duckula in amazement! 'See how the plants have grown!'

'But it's only a short time since we passed through,' said Igor. 'It's most strange. You can't even see what's inside now. The plants have taken over!'

Duckula was just as bewildered, but as he was feeling very clever lately, he thought of an explanation.

'Haven't you ever heard of . . . of plant sound response, Igor?'

'I can't say I have, milord.'

'Well, it works like this. The rustling of the plants must have set of the warning system, which, in turn, set off a reaction, causing the plants to grow quickly.'

'A curious and revolutionary phenomenon, milord.'

'It is, isn't it! Say, Igor, I could market it! I might become a millionaire . . . and *famous* as well!'

'Quite so, sir.'

'Igor, is that all the enthusiasm you can muster? This is world-shattering, you know!'

'I wonder how the leaves could have rustled, milord. There's no wind in the conservatory.'

'No, but there's plenty of wind in *you*, Igor. You're an old windbag. You're a damp squib! Always throwing cold water on my inventions and plans!'

'I'm a realist, milord.'

'Is that what you call yourself? I can think of a few

other names! Now let's keep going. We're never going to find Nanny at this rate.'

Duckula's electronic warning system had to be left behind in the conservatory. They hadn't quite got the means to cut through the tangled greenery to reach it! Actually, Duckula wasn't too sorry to leave his system behind. It was getting a bit tiresome, running back to move it along every few minutes!

They decided to return to the great hall and spy on Mitch and Ed. Duckula was getting very impatient to solve the mystery!

14
Finding Out!

Back in Castle Duckula, the bats were wondering how the absent residents were getting on. Much as they complained about Duckula and made fun of him, they were really quite fond of the little Count.

'Hey, Sviatoslav, I've heard there's going to be a few changes around Windup Manor since the duck and company moved in!' called Dmitri.

Sviatoslav shot out from his side of the clock. 'Really, my friend. Such as?'

'The ghosts are moving out! They took one look at Igor and decided they couldn't stand the competition!'

The clock shook with peals of bat laughter.

'C'mon Igor, let's peep in . . .' Duckula popped his head round the doorway of the great hall.

There was no one to be seen. Mitch and Ed had obviously gone looking for Nanny or Charlie . . . or something. Duckula and Igor tiptoed in. Everywhere was still and silent, except for a strange whirring sound.

'What's that noise?' whispered Duckula.

'The tape-recorder, milord.'

'Of course, Igor! Let's play it back and see if we learn anything.'

'Rather risky, don't you think?' replied Igor.

'We'll turn the sound low and keep looking out. If anyone comes, we'll . . . well, we'll hide somewhere.'

'Where, sir?'

'What?'

'Where will we hide?'

'I don't know. Yes I do! We'll hide behind this sofa. Unless it's Nanny, of course!' Duckula thought Igor invented problems sometimes!

They had to listen very carefully to catch the conversation between the dreadful duo, but what they heard was certainly worth listening to!

At first, it wasn't very interesting; just talk about sending Charlie to look for Nanny and discussing what they'd like to do with Duckula and Igor when they caught up with them.

Duckula knelt by the machine, tense with anticipation. The first tasty bit of gossip concerned Charlie.

'Hope Charlie survives tackling that big hen,' laughed Mitch. 'Sooner him than me!'

'She's a weighty sheila all right!' came the other's voice, followed by a slurping sound as he took a swig of lemonade. 'Good idea of mine to fool Charlie like that! Fancy him believing we were looking for the lost goodies to give to old Lady Windup so she could afford to stay here and grow peculiar plants! What a crazy cuckoo he is!'

'Hear that?' whispered Duckula.

'Yes, milord. It appears we've done . . . hmm . . . Good-Time Charlie an injustice.'

The tape continued with Mitch saying, 'When you wrote and told me you were coming home from down under, I knew you'd have something up your sleeve . . . like that duck's Nanny always has something up her sling!'

Ed could then be heard answering, 'Well, after that old sheep farmer told me the story that'd been handed down from his great-great-great-grandfather, I had to do something. Yer know me, Mitch . . . I don't let the grass grow under me feet! Not that there's much grass in the outback!'

This was intriguing stuff! '*What* story?' hissed Duckula, as if the machine could hear him.

Mitch was talking now. 'But when you told me I had to get a job at Windup Manor, I wasn't sure I'd manage it! Not with my record, anyway! What self-respecting lord would want a bank robber as a butler? Lucky he didn't ask for references!'

Igor's face darkened at this revelation. The rogue was giving butlers a bad name!

Duckula, was getting increasingly excited. What more information would these two laughing, scornful villains reveal? How fortunate that the wicked pair had forgotten about the tape-recorder!

Then, for a very short time, things went quiet. The silence lasted only a few seconds, but it was long enough for Duckula to almost scream with frustration. Wasn't he about to discover what was going on after all?

He needn't have worried! Ed began to boast about his adventures in Australia and, after a lot of recollections of how he'd boxed with kangaroos, wrestled with alligators, ridden wild horses, climbed sheer rock faces, survived days in the desert without food or water, recovered from poisonous snake bites, swum in infested rivers, mined for gold and so and so on and so on, he got onto the important part!

86

All through the tales of daring and adventure, Igor had been tutting in disbelief and muttering things like, 'A likely story!' and, 'Tall tales, if you ask me!' and, 'I don't believe a word!' and 'Utterly impossible!'

As for Duckula, he'd been secretly enthralled by the stories, though he wouldn't admit that to Igor, of course!

Now Ed came to the story which went something like this: he met this very, very old sheep farmer. When the old boy heard that Ed came from England, he asked him if he knew of an English stately home called Windup Manor. Ed didn't, but was curious why the old farmer wanted to know. It turned out that, many years before, the old farmer's ancestor, Sam Luckless, had been in service at Windup Manor as a junior footman.

Sam hadn't been at the place very long, and was fascinated by the endless rooms and corridors in the huge house. He'd only lived in a tiny hovel with his parents and lots of brothers and sisters, and this was such a change. In his few hours off duty, Sam liked nothing better than to explore. He'd heard tales of secret passages and longed to find one himself. No one else seemed to know how to. The passages were all part of the legend of Windup Manor – like the supposed ghosts – but nobody except Sam could be bothered to find out. Not even the Lord and Lady Windup of that time.

Sam guessed that the library probably contained at least one way into a secret passage, and he was right! A bit of pushing and prodding and one of the shelves opened up. In went Sam who was soon exploring the warren of passages. He was very pleased with himself. In fact, he got carried away, wandered off a bit too far and got himself lost!

What a job he had trying to find his way back to the library. He made lots of wrong turnings and one of them proved his undoing! It led into a small, dark alcove. Sam was just about to turn back again when something sparkling caught his eye. He looked closer and to his amazement he saw it was a large diamond ring. And there were other things too: jewels, trinkets, letters, documents . . . bits and pieces like that.

Sam took the ring to show Lady Windup. It took him ages to find his way back to the library. When he finally did get back and washed all the dust and cobwebs off himself, he was late for his duties. He put the ring down in his room and forgot about it while he was working. But one of the other servants recognised it as being Lady Windup's most valuable and favourite diamond ring. It had gone missing from her dressing table. This servant couldn't get to Her Lady-ship fast enough to tell her about the ring in Sam's room. Poor Sam hadn't had time to tell her, of course.

Naturally, when Sam was confronted by Lady Windup, he explained and told her all about the other things down in the passage. It turned out that many other valuables were missing from Lady Windup's room.

Sam went back down to find the hidden place but, try as he might, he couldn't. Other servants went with him . . . even Lord Windup went down, but no one succeeded in finding the hoard of treasures. In the end, they just didn't believe him. He was charged with stealing not only the ring but all the rest of the missing items and, as often happened in those days, he was deported to Australia.

That, more or less, was how Ed told the story, and it left Duckula and Igor spellbound. No doubt about it – they'd stumbled on a *real* adventure!

15

Tales of Deception!

'So that's why Ed came here . . . and why he told his old friend to get a job here . . . and that's why he lied to Charlie – to find the hidden riches!' exclaimed Duckula.

The tape-recording wasn't finished yet!

'Poor Sam!' Mitch could be heard saying sarcastically. 'Wasn't there something about his violin?'

'That's right!' answered Ed. 'When he was deported, Sam had to leave behind not only his country, but his treasured violin. He loved playin' that fiddle. It'd been handed down in his family. He really missed it and never managed to buy another one during his lifetime down under. Shame! But never mind – his bad luck'll be our good luck! When I heard the tale, I made me mind up to find that stuff down underneath this old place. That was unless it already had been found. Once you'd started working for Lord Windup and asked a few nosy little questions, you soon found out that the stuff must still be there, just waiting to be found!

'And with us being so alike, I could stand in while you were moochin' around the cellars looking for the loot. The old goat Windup never realised that I wasn't you. Not even with my Australian accent . . . he just thought you'd been watching too many TV soaps! I imagined we'd find the stuff in two shakes of a kangaroos's tail. Next step was to think of a way to get old Lord and Lady Windup and all the rest of the servants out of the way so we could really search without anyone bothering us.'

Mitch was laughing. 'And once I'd got Charlie on my side, it was easy to rustle up a few nice ghosts to empty the place. I didn't bargain for the newspapers interfering, calling it "the most haunted house in the country" and putting this idiotic duck in. The spotlight's on the place now and we've got to be careful.'

'The public can't resist a good ghost story!' boomed Ed. 'And we certainly gave them a good selection of ghosts! Remember when you covered yourself in a white sheet and snatched His Lordship's gold watch?'

Guffaws of laughter bellowed from the tape-recorder, followed by Mitch saying, 'Serves the old miser right. He should pay me better wages! Hey, I've just thought of something . . . you don't think that violin music we've been hearing could be . . .?'

'Nah!' was the other's swift response. 'There's no such thing as real spooks! It must have been a radio outside somewhere . . . or Charlie or someone else playing a joke on us. This house seems to be full of nosy parkers right now. That duck brought his servants, and who knows what other snoopers might be creepin' about!'

'The duck's butler and his Nanny are ugly enough to scare any spooks off!' said Mitch.

'And I wish that whoever's playin' that fiddle would learn a few decent tunes!' said Ed.

Then the voices trailed off as the wicked duo decided they were both feeling peckish and left the great hall, presumably to head in the direction of the kitchens . . .

Duckula's eyes shone with excitement. Igor, on the other hand, wore a rather downcast expression. He might have expected that the young master would get mixed up in dangerous escapades like this! It was simply the way things always turned out. Duckula had a taste for adventure that Igor couldn't share. Now, a taste for *blood* . . . that'd be a different matter entirely!

'You know what we must do, don't you, Igor?' asked Duckula eagerly. 'Find the secret passage and the valuable things that Sam was blamed for stealing.'

'I thought you'd say that, milord,' sighed Igor. 'We also have to find Nanny, remember.'

'Oh . . . yes, naturally. We must find Nanny, too. But don't you see, Igor . . . if we can find that hidden stuff before the horrible pair do, we can return it to the rightful owners, Lord and Lady Windup. They'll be able to afford to keep this house and they'll be so pleased to know it's not really haunted! Lady Windup will be able to start her plant project . . . whatever it is . . . and, best of all, Sam's name will be cleared; not that it'll do him much good now. The old sheep farmer in Australia will be grateful to us, though. In fact, everyone will be. We'll be famous, Igor!'

'I have never courted fame, milord,' replied Igor, drily.

'Oh, you are a wet blanket, Igor.'

'I've been told I have a rather *dry* humour,' said Igor. 'Shall we make haste?'

'Yes, we'd better,' agreed Duckula. He was feeling

terribly hungry now, what with all the excitement and anticipation of the events ahead. Why, one of the villains had even eaten his sandwiches! 'Shall we go down to the kitchens and see if we can get anything to eat. A cucumber sandwich and a cream bun would go down a treat!'

'I think not, milord. Unless we wish to meet up with the evil creatures.'

'Mmm, you're right again, Igor! What would I do without you?

'Precisely the question I ask myself, milord.'

'I was only joking, Igor. I could manage very well on my own . . . so watch your manners or you'll be looking for another job! Say, I think Lord Windup will be advertising for a replacement butler soon!' giggled Duckula.

'Might I suggest that it's not my manners I should be watching but . . . hmmm . . . Mitch Manners and his crude accomplice who are probably on their way back here at this very moment.'

Duckula frowned. He decided he'd have to take Igor down a peg or two!

At the far end of the hall was another door. This seemed to be the safest exit in the circumstances. Duckula's thinking was slightly cooler by this time and, with a stab of fear, he realised that this was no game – no publicity stunt. They were in real danger from real criminals, one of whom had travelled from the other side of the world to carry out his underhand activities.

Duckula breathed deeply and stuck out his chest boldly. It was his awesome responsibility to protect the innocent parties in this matter and bring the wrongdoers to justice. Oh, but if only he could have a cup of Nanny's cocoa and a slice of marzipan cake it'd all be so much easier! It is hard to be heroic when you're famished!

16

Bloomin' Nanny

As it turned out, Mitch and Ed's visit to the kitchen was not without unexpected incident, for they found somebody already there. An extremely angry goose-like character to be exact!

'Heinrich, I am never being so . . . so full of zee fury!' cried the irate Doctor. 'Zee idiot of a ninny is off on a run-away tea-trolley. Zat is not so important, you might sink, but my latest wampire-waporiser – zee quantum-leap in wampire-destroying advances, an ultra-efficient-hands-on-technology super-sophisticated piece of equipment – is run away wiz her!

'Vhat can I do, Heinrich? It is distraught I am. Vhat do you say? Ja, I am agreeing wiz you . . . I must catch zee tea-trolley und retrieve mine machine. I am just hoping zat it is not damaged. Zen, I can carry out mine mission to rid zee vorld of zee wampire Dugula. I dream of zat day, Heinrich. At last I vill be able to be enjoying zee hobbies like everyone else. I might get a canoe wiz a paddle, or perhaps a bicycle!'

Mitch and Ed stood in the kitchen doorway and watched in surprise as Von Goosewing carried on!

'Hee-hee!' he chuckled to his imaginary friend. 'You'll never believe ziss, but in mine university days I vas a very gut tennis player!' Inspired by the memories of his youth, he plucked a very ripe tomato from the vegetable rack and, with a half-turn of his body and a little leap in the air, gave it a hefty lob. A fraction too late, the unlucky doctor noticed his curious observers.

'Splosh!' The tomato landed slap on Ed's forehead, causing the corks on his hat to dangle wildly.

'What on earth . . .?' began the furious Ed, as the squashed tomato began to slide down his face.

'Who are you and what are you doing here?' roared Mitch.

'I . . . I am sorry,' spluttered a very embarrassed Von Goosewing, his face turning nearly as red as Ed's.

'You've no right to be here, you stupid goose!' bellowed Ed, in between spitting out tomato seeds. 'I've a good mind to squash a whole barrel of tomatoes in your simpering mush and see how you like it!'

'I . . . I vas simply explaining zee game of tennis . . .' said Von Goosewing.

'Who to?' laughed Mitch. 'A ghost?' and the two roared with raucous laughter, as Von Goosewing became more and more flustered.

'I vas explaining to mine friend Heinrch . . .'

'Where is he?' asked Mitch.

'He must be invisible!' sneered Ed.

'Mind your own business!' snapped the doctor.

'Hey, don't take that tone with us, sport!' said Ed, the grin swiftly vanishing from his face. 'Tell us what you're doing here and be quick about it or you'll be sorry – and that's a promise.'

'I am Doctor Von Gooseving and I am here on top-secret research,' declared Goosewing.

'Hear that!' exclaimed Mitch. 'He's a doctor!'

'I wouldn't like him to give me an injection,' laughed the other. 'His aim's not too good!'

Von Goosewing felt foolish and humiliated. Who were this uncouth pair? How dare they make fun of him like this!

'I am a scientist . . . very clever . . . highly educated. So move out of mine vay, if you please.'

The villainous couple weren't going to let him off the hook *that* easily!

'I don't care if you've got more degrees than a thermometer!' snapped Mitch. 'Get out of the house and take your invisible friend with you!'

'I thought that duck was a load of trouble, but this goose is worse!' said Ed.

'Duck? *Duck?*' cried Von Goosewing.

'Why?' asked Ed. 'Are you plannin' to throw another tomato?'

Von Goosewing ignored this. He was now far too interested in the reference to the duck. 'Iss it zee evil Count Dugula you are talking about?' he asked eagerly.

'I don't know about evil,' sneered Mitch. 'But he's a diabolical nuisance!'

'Vhere is he? Tell me! I must find zee fiend!' cried the doctor. 'Tell me ziss instant!'

'We might and we might *not*!' teased Ed.

'We know where he is, all right,' lied Mitch. 'But we'll just have to think about whether to tell you or not.'

This was all too much for Von Goosewing. He lunged forward towards his tormentors, waving his wings madly, begging them to tell him.

Almost collapsing with laughter, the pair pushed him away . . . right into a sack of flour that promptly burst all over the place.

'Now *you* look like a ghost!' they roared.

Poor Nanny was having a terrible struggle fighting her way out of the conservatory. All she could see was a thick green mass . . . rather like her own greengage jelly, actually! In all the years Nanny had been making jelly, she'd never once managed to get the right proportion of jelly cubes to water. So the jelly either turned out like hard plastic that you couldn't even get a spoon into, or like soup so thin you could drink it through a straw!

To get back to the conservatory . . . what a pitiful sight! Nanny, lying on a tea-trolley, stuck in the midst of tangled, twisted greenery. If we'd been there perhaps we could have helped her, couldn't we? But never fear! Nanny had splintered the thickest of doors and the sturdiest of floorboards into smithereens in her time . . . so she surely wasn't going to be beaten by mere plants, leaves, flowers, ferns and shrubs.

With a tremendous effort, she heaved herself off the tea-trolley and freed her way through the overgrown flora. As she did, she talked to herself, saying things like: 'Oooh, what a performance! I likes a nice potted geranium but this is *ridiculous*!'

At last she was free! But you'd have hardly recognised her as good old Nanny! From head to toe, from one side to the other – and, let's face it – that's a lot of area! – was covered in sticky bits of leaves, grass, twigs and various other growths! Poor Nanny looked for all the world like an elephantine, green monster!

To make matters worse, Duckula's electronic warning system had stuck to one of the sticky leaves on Nanny's broad back! Although the device had become damaged in the turmoil, it wasn't entirely out of action! Every few minutes, it would suddenly emit a burst of the high-pitched warning sound.

Each time this happened, Nanny, not realising that the thing was attached to her, turned round as fast as someone of her size and in her predicament could, and shouted, 'Who's that, blowin' a whistle behind me back?'

Nanny was very cross! It was bad enough having to walk through the house with virtually a whole forest stuck to your body without having to put up with someone whistling behind your back every few minutes!

'Now, just stop it!' she called, trying to turn round quickly enough to see the prankster. There certainly didn't seem to be anyone there at all . . . no footsteps . . . nothing . . . nobody . . . except . . . 'Oh no!' cried Nanny. 'A whistlin' spook!' And she hurried along as fast as she could, dropping odd leaves like a huge oak tree in autumn. The noise carried on, too. Whenever she thought she'd shaken the thing off, it let out a terrifying shriek! Nanny was utterly miserable. If only she could find Duckyboos and get out of this awful house!

17
Sorry Sights and Sneezes!

Mitch and Ed were still sniggering as they left the kitchen to continue their search for what had now become a whole collection of things: Duckula and Igor, Nanny, Charlie . . . not forgetting the lost booty.

'We sure floured him!' giggled Ed. 'What a ridiculous sight!'

'Ideal look for a haunted house!' agreed Mitch. 'Makes it seem more genuine. Hey, maybe there is something in this publicity stunt after all! How about trying to cheat old Windup out of this dump and opening it up as a tourist attraction! Old Goosegrease could be the star turn!'

The beastly partners in crime laughed their way to the great hall.

You won't be surprised to learn that Goosewing wasn't so amused! In fact, he was blazing with fury! The flour was all over him . . . even down his ears! He looked like a piece of dough, ready for the oven!

Shaking himself and trying to brush the flour off just made him sneeze. 'Achoo! Achoo! Zee horrible creatures! How *dare* they do ziss to me. It iss an insult. It is degrading. How can I carry on mine waluable wampire-destroying vork when I am leaving flour trails all over zee place? I haff ein gut mind to invent a machine to deal wiz zem! Next time they'll get more than a tomato!'

A sudden noise startled him. It seemed to be coming from the larder. He walked over and listened. Were the pair of look-alike magpies coming back? He became agitated at the prospect. He'd like to be ready for them . . . he'd like to be, but he wasn't, of course!

The noise got louder. Von Goosewing opened the larder door. It was as if someone was trying to push through the wall at the back. How strange. Why would anyone want to do that? Then he was astounded to see the wall swing open, just like a door, and two very dirty, exhausted professors came tumbling through.

Von Goosewing gasped and stepped back several inches, flour flying from him in all directions. What a bizarre trio they made: Von Goosewing's funny shape completely covered in flour, with just his eyes, wide with bewilderment and confusion, shining out from his face and giving him a ghastly look – and the two professors, cobwebs hanging from their hair, the dust of centuries clinging to their clothes, their frightened eyes blinking in the half-light.

The learned pair's relief at finally breaking out of the secret passage was short-lived, for this creature with its deadly pallor was surely a ghost.

'Help!' they cried, pushing past the astonished Von Goosewing. It was all too much for them. Their encounter with the gigantic hen had put paid to their ghost-hunting once and for all. After their long ordeal they were in no state to tackle this white apparition!

After his initial shock at the professors' appearance, Von Goosewing was quite relieved. Maybe these two would help him to get his revenge on the magpies and find Duckula! He didn't consider the possibility that they might be ghosts. Unlike them, he hadn't come to the haunted house to ghost-hunt, but to hunt down a vampire. In his book, a vampire was far deadlier than *any* spook!

Dafty and Owlie were desperate to get away, running and stumbling over chairs and tables and slipping on the remains of the squashed tomato.

'Come back, if you please!' called Von Goosewing. 'I am in need of zee help!'

'It's the notorious snow spectre, I'll be bound!' panted Dafty. 'As reported in *Spooks Spotted In Arctic Circles* by Ferdinand Frostbite, fellow in psychical research at the Igloo Institute of Idiotic Studies.'

'D'you think so?' gasped Owlie. 'I fancied it might be Ted the baker who's supposed to return to haunt his old kitchens. They say that occasionally, after Ted's visited, you can even smell the bread baking. Though I must say he didn't look like a very efficient baker to me! More flour on him than in the mixing bowl!'

'No, I'll wager it's the snow spectre,' puffed Dafty. The main thing is that we *escape* it!'

Off they ran, with a very uncomfortable and frequently sneezing Von Goosewing in hot and floury pursuit!

Doctor Von Goosewing wasn't the only one who was having a ticklish time: that walking, sixteen-stone botanical garden – otherwise known as Nanny – was experiencing the same trouble! The abundance of flora in such close proximity to her nose had well and truly set off her hay fever!

Unfortunately, whenever she sneezed . . . and don't forget that a hearty sneeze from Nanny is akin to a blast from a Force 10 gale . . . she also set off the electronic warning system which was still stuck to her back!

'Oooh, I'm proper fed up!' she moaned as she waddled along the corridor leading to the library. 'I've . . . atchoo! . . . got a tickly nose . . . atchoo! And that ghost is still whistlin' at me!'

Nanny did have some of her hay fever medicine in her sling at the time . . . actually, she'd had hay fever medicine in her sling for a century or two . . . but she couldn't get at it. The sling was too full of sticky leaves and spiky twigs!

And on top of all this, she still couldn't find Duckula and was getting very worried about him. She hoped against hope that a ghost hadn't got him. These ghosts seemed so cheeky, what with the two chimney sweep spooks who wanted to feed her to their dog and this one who kept following her and whistling when she least expected it.

Her little Duckyboos would be no match for such tricky phantoms, she thought. She wondered whether he'd eaten those sandwiches yet. As for Igor, she was disgusted with him . . . leaving her all alone to face those two spooks. It wasn't fair! She decided to give him a piece of her mind when she met up with him again . . . if she ever did. Oh no, I mustn't think like that, she told herself.

She sang a little song to cheer herself up. 'La la tra

la tra . . .' Then s-c-r-e-e-c-h! There it went again, that awful sound!

'Stop whistlin'!' she cried. 'An' stop followin' me! Ah-choo!'

It was no wonder that Nanny felt weary, and who could blame her when she decided not to carry on towards the library but to drag her tired bulk upstairs in the hope of having a nice lie down in a comfy bed?

Little did she know that she *wasn't* going to find much rest there!

18

Ghost in a Basket?

'Oh, me poor feet!' sighed Nanny, eyeing a large, four-poster bed. Surely no one would mind if she snatched forty winks? After all, she'd had a traumatic night!

Flop! she went on the bed – and shriek went the dreadful sound. Because she was lying on her back and pressing on the device, the noise wouldn't stop.

'Oh no! The whistlin' ghost is under the bed now!' she cried. 'Get out and leave me alone! Go an' whistle at somebody else!'

She heaved herself into a sitting-up position and the noise stopped at once. What a relief! Down she lay . . . and it started again! The 'ghost' had made such a nuisance of itself that Nanny's initial fear of it had been replaced by anger. But what could she do to get rid of it? Nothing, it seemed. With a good deal of effort, she manoeuvred herself on to her side, hoping to shut out some of the sound with the pillows. Then, to her delight, all went silent!

If Nanny had decided to go into the library she'd have found Duckula and Igor there, pacing the floor and gazing around in bewilderment. From what they had heard on the tape, the library was clearly the place to look for the way into the secret passage. But where should they start? Every wall was lined with books.

Thousands of them on every subject under the sun, and lying around on desks and tables were lots of volumes on rare plants and suchlike; obviously Lady Windup's favourite reading of the moment.

Duckula thought most of the books were pretty boring, except, possibly the ones about electronics, though even these spoiled themselves by using long words. Duckula's reading habits were mostly confined to comics! Why anyone should want to read a big book with all words and no pictures was beyond him!

'We'll stay here till we find the secret passage!' he told Igor.

'Milord, may I remind you that we have only about three hours before the loosely termed "gentlemen of the press" will be descending on this house to discover how you fared?'

'What?' spluttered Duckula in surprise. He'd almost forgotten why he'd come to Windup Manor in the first place! Igor's reminder made him think quickly. There was no time to lose! They began frantically pulling out books and feeling around the backs of the shelves.

'Zzzz . . . zzzz!' snored Nanny and with every snore the bed vibrated and the centuries-old bedposts creaked. Yet Nanny wasn't sleeping peacefully. A strange rustling and bumping noise kept disturbing her slumbers. After a particularly loud bump, Nanny opened her eyes and in her half-sleep she imagined she was back home in the Castle.

'What is it, Duckyboos? Are you 'avin' a bad

dream? Nanny'll bring you a cup o' warm milk an' a custard cream biscuit. Ooh, where *am* I?'

Once Nanny had realised where she was, she became quite frightened and annoyed, too. If she wasn't being troubled by a whistling ghost, spooky chimney sweeps and sticky plants, she was being woken up by . . . she looked around the room and nearly fell out of the bed at the sight of . . . a walking linen basket!

Walking wasn't really the right word. The basket was actually jumping, trundling and scuttling frantically around the bedroom floor. Nanny gazed in wonder. Not a ghost in a basket, surely! Whatever *next*?!

Nanny was about to leave – she'd had enough ghostly experiences to last her several lifetimes! – when she heard a faint voice coming from the basket.

'Help! Please help me! Get me out!'

Now, as you well know, Nanny is a soft-hearted soul who never could resist a genuine plea for help from almost anyone or anything in difficulties . . . even a walking linen basket!

'Who are you?' she asked. 'Are you a spook?'

'No, of course I'm not! What a time to ask me such a thing! I'm Good-Time Charlie, Lord Windup's footman.'

Nanny vaguely remembered meeting Charlie at the cottage, but the events of the previous few hours seemed all jumbled up in her head. Mind you, things in Nanny's head were usually jumbled up anyway!

'All right, I'll let you out,' said Nanny, opening the

basket. 'I daresay I shouldn't, but I'm a fool to meself!'

Charlie jumped out of the basket with glee! He was very grateful to Nanny and thanked her profusely, which made her warm to him. What a nice cuckoo, she thought, and it gave her a nice feeling, rescuing someone.

And when Charlie explained who'd shut him in the basket, Nanny had plenty to say!

'My little Duckyboos did it? He must 'ave been up to 'is silly games . . .'e loves 'ide an' seek. Fancy forgettin' to let you out, the young scamp. I'll only give 'im *one* chocolate wafer instead o' two, when I find 'im!'

'I didn't mind at first,' Charlie explained. 'But I did think they'd come back and let me out after a time.'

'The little rascal . . . Achoo! Oh, me sneezin's startin' again, but at least the whistlin's gone!'

Charlie looked puzzled. 'Er, bless you,' he said. 'Duckyboos – I mean, your master, Count Duckula – has made enemies for all time of Mitch Manners, the butler and his partner, Ed Eyesore. I don't know why, because they're only trying to help Lord Windup.'

Now Nanny was utterly confused. Her brainpower had its limitations, after all! ''Ow were you goin' to 'elp Lord Windythingy?'

'Well, it's a long story. I haven't got time to tell you all about it, but the first thing we have to do is find the secret passage. By the way, madam, why are you covered in leaves and things?'

'I . . . I was on a tea-trolley and . . . ooh, that's a

108

long story as well. Tell me about the secret passage. Is it long an' dark an' 'orrible?'

'I . . . I expect so.'

'I've been in it!' Nanny declared, proudly.

'You have?'

'Yes! I was chased through it by two chimney sweep spooks who wanted to feed me to their dog. The nerve!'

Charlie had given up trying to make sense of most of what Nanny had to say, but could she *really* have found the secret passage?

'Please take me to the passage!' he begged, imagining what a triumph it'd be for him to find the passage before Mitch and Ed, who were always bossing him about. He'd become so fed up with their attitude lately that he'd been tempted to stop working for them. But he'd do anything to help Lady Windup make a success of her project. What he didn't quite understand was why the magpies, who seemed so greedy, wanted to help. It had occurred to him that they wanted to find the lost loot for themselves, but he'd put these thoughts out of his mind. Charlie always liked to think the best of everyone. Still, he'd keep a sharp eye on them!

Nanny was trying to think back to how she came to be in the secret passage. 'Was it in the library? No, that's where I came out . . . or was it where I went in? Let me think . . . it could 'ave been when I went in the bathroom . . . or was it the kitchen?'

She and Charlie both sat on the linen basket while she thought.

Suddenly, she remembered. 'The *larder*!' she cried,

leaping up and down on the basket, causing the floorboard . . . or rather, the trap door, to give way and send the basket, Charlie and Nanny down . . . down . . . down the secret staircase. The basket went ahead of them, breaking their fall. They landed in a twisted heap, bits of wicker basket and sticky leaves everywhere . . . and the terrible whistling sound echoing in the gloom.

Charlie was glad he'd found the secret passage, though he would have preferred an easier route!

19
A Floury Battle!

Duckula and Igor weren't having much luck in the library.

'I'm fed up!' cried Duckula, pulling one book after another from the shelves in frustration.

Soon there were piles of books lying around the floor. Igor had made himself comfortable in an armchair and was deeply interested in a big book entitled *A Creepy Collection of Horror Stories*.

'Igor, you *might* give me a hand!' yelled Duckula.

But Igor was too engrossed. '. . . and the slimy creature slid up from the cellar and poised to attack . . .' he read.

'Igor! Stop!' The gruesome tale was making Duckula's feathers tingle with fear.

'Sorry, milord. I was quite carried away. What a *superior* work of literature this is.'

Duckula was unimpressed. 'Never mind that. Help me find the secret passage. We've not got much time left.'

But Igor was sceptical. 'Surely if a secret passage existed we would have found it by now.'

All this banter had prevented either of them hearing someone approaching the library. Too late, the door burst open to reveal a ghastly figure, rather like a battered, chalky statue, come to life! Von Goosewing, of course!

On seeing the dumbfounded Duckula, the doctor's eyes, looking like dark holes in the pale face, blazed with sudden excitement.

'Dugula!' he cried. '*At last!*'

Shocked, Duckula stood still, as if rooted to the floor, a book held in midair. 'A *ghost*,' he murmured. A ghost who knew his name, although it pronounced it strangely!

Igor didn't hesitate. He'd heard that voice before and knew at once it meant great danger to his beloved master.

'*Escape*, milord!' he cried. 'This is none other than Doctor Von Goosewing, an enemy more dedicated to your destruction than any mere ghost!'

Duckula gasped and dropped the book in terror. What could he do? Where could he escape to? His back was literally against the wall, or, to be exact, against the book shelf. He instinctively stepped back . . . and back . . . and back . . .

Igor had never been so motivated. Down through the centuries he had protected the Duckula dynasty and though the present Count Duckula had proved a great disappointment, Igor's loyalty was no less. Whatever had to be done to protect the young master would *be* done. His face – never pretty at the best of times – was set like a mask, grim with determination, his eyes cold as steel, his thin-lipped mouth tight with defiance.

But action, not attitude was needed now! Igor grabbed a large vase of flowers and threw the water all over the flour-covered enemy. The library, like the rest of Windup Manor, contained plenty of flowers, so there were lots more soakings in store for the unfortunate doctor!

'S-p-l-a-s-h!' went another; 'slurp' went yet another!

Well, if you thought Von Goosewing was in a mess before, you should have seen him after he'd been watered! The mixture of flour and water became a sort of horrid, sticky dough! It was even yuckier than Nanny's dough when she rolled pastry to make apple pies. On those occasions the walls in the Castle kitchen looked a bit like Von Goosewing did at this moment.

'Get out of my vay, you oaf,' yelled the furious doctor. 'Zee fiend's servants mess up my plans and mess me up too! I am vet and sludgy all over. Your fat colleague, zee silly Ninny, vent off vith my wampire-waporiser on zee tea-trolley. I vill haff to rely on my portable pocket wersion. It is not zo powerful but in zee circumstances I haff no choice. It iss better zan nothing . . . und viz any luck, *you*, my ugly creature, vill soon haff no master!'

Von Goosewing tried to retrieve his miniature vampire-vaporiser from his pocket, but it was a hopeless task. All his pockets were filled with wet dough!

He finally managed to find the little machine and desperately pulled at the greyish mass covering it. Some of the dough came off in long strings, but the device was obviously ruined.

'You haff clogged it up, you monster! It iss a delicate, sensitive instrument, not suitable for zee attack by zee flour and vater. Count Dugula and his clumsy servants are an affront to modern technolgy. Zhey belong in zee Stone Age . . . or, better still, they belong in *no* age at all!'

Von Goosewing was so angry, he lost his tenuous grip on the wet floor and went sliding along on his back, coming to a dazed halt in the middle of a pile of books.

'I did rather *well*, didn't I, milord?' asked Igor, turning to Duckula – but his master wasn't there! He glanced around the library. Only rows and rows of books could be seen. There was no other door. Had Duckula found the secret passage at last? Well, what do *you* think?

Of course Duckula *had* found the secret passage! More by accident than design, but never mind, he was in it, and that was the important thing! A gloomy and miserable place it was too!

When he'd leaned back against the book shelf in fear of Von Goosewing, a complete section of shelving had simply swung aside and he'd tumbled down what was left of the rope ladder – the very place where Nanny had left the passage and stumbled into the library after being pursued by the two professors!

By the way, have you been wondering what happened to that clever duo? Despite their academic qualifications, they weren't very bright in other ways. For one thing, they were still in Windup Manor! Believing that the white ghost – really Von Goosewing, of course – was chasing them, they were in hiding. That is, if you can call being hunched up behind a sofa in hiding. Not a smart move, especially when Mitch Manners and Ed Eyesore were about! But, like I said, the professors weren't very smart!

★ ★, ★

Now, what was Duckula up to in that dismal underground world? The answer is – not very much! After picking himself up and realising where he was, he didn't know whether to laugh or cry. He was still shaking from his near miss with danger from Von Goosewing, yet he couldn't help but be delighted that he'd found the secret passage. If only he weren't all alone. He was missing Nanny terribly and now he didn't even have Igor's company. Not that Igor was very cheerful company, but the faithful old retainer had certainly shown his devotion in the confrontation with the enemy!

Duckula began to wander along the narrow, winding passage. It was an eerie place. In the parts where the walls weren't lamplit, it was very dark and Duckula had left his torch behind in the library. The camera was slung around his neck, however – *not* that he'd had any chance to use it yet.

Now and then, a shrill noise made him stop in his tracks. It was rather like the sound made by his electronic ghost-warning system.

Soon, the weary little duck had to rest. He sank down to the cold stone floor and sat there, his back leaning against the damp wall. He wasn't used to being alone, especially in a secret passage in a haunted house. The novelty of finding the passage was wearing off and he felt utterly desolate. He had no idea what was happening up above, in the house . . . he didn't even know what time it was. The Castle might have already flown back to Transylvania!

There was some serious thinking to be done; something Duckula wasn't used to. His serious thinking usually extended to whether to have tomato ketchup or chutney on his broccoli sandwiches.

Should he go back to the library? He doubted whether he could find his way back. And how about Von Goosewing? No, there was only one course of honourable action:

'I'll find the hidden jewels, or whatever it is, all by myself!' he declared aloud. '*By myself . . . by myself . . .*' his vow echoed down the chilly passage.

20
Sam's Place!

'Duckyboos! Is that you?'

Never had Duckula been so happy to hear his Nanny's voice! She'd heard his voice echoing and, followed by Charlie, rushed to find her precious charge.

'Nanny!' called Duckula, leaping up from his sitting position and running towards her, only to skid to a stop in surprise. Was this thing really his dear, lovable Nanny? It looked more like a huge walking forest!

Nanny gave Duckula such a big hug it almost squeezed all the breath out of him, not to mention covering him with sticky, ticklish leaves. At the same time, a terrible screeching noise came from Nanny's body. Duckula knew that sound. It was his electronic warning system! After a few seconds, the noise stopped.

'What's *happened* to you?' Duckula asked. 'You've turned into a tree!'

'Don't be so bloomin' cheeky!' said Nanny, pretending to be cross. She did her best to explain, which left Duckula none the wiser! And what, he asked, was she doing with his electronic warning system?

'*I've* not got your electric cistern,' she said. 'Cisterns is only in bathrooms. Why would I walk about with one? I'd get wet!'

'It was making that noise just then . . . and there it goes again!' yelled Duckula.

'Take no notice of it!' shouted Nanny. 'It might go away!'

'What?'

'I said it might go away if you ignore it!' screamed Nanny at the top of her voice. 'It's the whistlin' ghost. There! It's stopped. I *told* you it would!'

'That's no *ghost*!' With an almighty tug, Duckula pulled his machine free. 'It's damaged, but I might be able to mend it.'

Nanny was astonished. To think that the whistling ghost *wasn't* a ghost at all!

It was time to explain everything to Charlie. As quickly as he could, Duckula told him all he and Igor had discovered about his 'friends', Mitch and Ed. Charlie had suspected something was wrong and was dismayed to think he'd helped to betray Lord and Lady Windup.

'I'll make it up to them by helping you!' he told Duckula.

'Great!' replied the now cheerful Count. 'But we haven't got much time. Say, isn't that your line?'

Problem now was where to look for the hidden store of goodies. Duckula plumped for going down a narrower passage which went off at right angles to the main one. This way wasn't quite as well lit, but he didn't care. He had renewed energy now and he was determined to find the mysterious hidden room.

The eager Count hurried on ahead so fast that Charlie and Nanny – especially Nanny – had trouble keeping up with him, and before long they had lost sight of him altogether.

He tapped on the walls, saying, 'D'you think it

could be a secret door or something?' and, 'I'm sure we must be close,' and, 'You might offer an opinion. I might as well be talking to myself. Oh no! I *am* talking to myself!'

How infuriating! He'd been so pleased to meet up with Nanny, even if she had got herself done up like a tree in full bloom. And now he was alone – again!

'That's it!' he yelled. 'I've had *enough*! D'you hear me anyone? Any vampires, Nannies, ghosts, geese . . . *enough*!'

Off he marched, roughly in the direction he imagined was the way out. Straight ahead! No looking round, no tapping on walls, he decided. Why should he do everything himself? Oh . . . and he was feeling scared again!

Then he heard it . . . violin music, sweet, tuneful . . . and very near. Despite his fear, he stopped and listened, as if hypnotised. The music seemed to be coming from one side of the passage wall, a little way ahead. At first glance the wall looked solid as it was in dark shadow, but when Duckula crept closer, he was surprised to find a tiny opening, a mere chink in the thick stone.

Amazingly for a not-very-brave duck who'd just lost his Nanny, Duckula squeezed through. He smiled to himself as he did so, thinking that Nanny would never get through such a narrow gap, anyway.

Duckula's heart was beating fast! He knew, without a doubt, that he'd found Sam's lost place! All was silent. The music had stopped. Had he been imagining it, he wondered.

The little room was completely hidden, yet,

strangely, it wasn't completely dark. Even without a torch, Duckula could see fairly well. And what remarkable sights were to be seen!

Scattered around the floor were all kinds of things. Not only valuable items like rings, necklaces, brooches and other trinkets, but also everyday items: combs, handkerchiefs, a little mirror, letters, bills, envelopes dating from different periods in history. Some were important-looking documents like deeds and others were just domestic items like grocery lists. What a strange mixture! And they were all gathering dust down under the house!

Duckula was bewildered. Surely no one *stole* all this stuff? He looked around and up and down – and as he looked up, he realised the answer was right there, above him! A chink of light was shining in through a gap high above the tiny cavern. The things had *fallen* down!

That was it! This place must be directly under the bedroom that the Lady Windups of the time had used. And he imagined that the present Lady Windup probably used the same bedroom. And that was most likely the bedroom with the grand four-poster where he'd put Charlie into the linen basket!

Duckula was triumphant! He couldn't wait to tell everyone, but he didn't like to leave the place somehow. Supposing, like poor Sam, he couldn't find it again. Then he had a dazzling idea! He'd take a photograph, using the electronic flash!

This done, it was time to leave. Now, where were Nanny and Charlie?

★ ★ ★

120

Fact is, these two hadn't had as much luck as Duckula. Once they'd lost him in the passage they'd retraced their steps and climbed up the stairs and back into the bedroom through the trap-door.

Poor Nanny was distraught at losing her Duckyboos again after only just finding him, but at least she'd solved the mystery of the whistling ghost!

Kindly Charlie tried to console her. 'Duckula will be all right. It was no use your staying down there, all covered in leaves. You were having a terrible time moving through the narrow passage. Come with me to the kitchen and I'll make you a nice cup of tea.'

Now it wasn't very often that anyone offered to make Nanny tea, so she accepted gratefully. Besides, she was tired and thirsty.

But Nanny wasn't to taste the fragrant steaming brew she was looking forward to. The path to the kitchen was blocked by the two leering faces of Mitch and Ed.

'Thought you'd doublecross us?' growled Mitch, to Charlie.

' I . . . I . . .' began Charlie, but he wasn't allowed to say anything before he and Nanny were marched into the great hall and ordered to sit down, stay still and shut up!

They weren't the only prisoners either! Sitting glumly on one chair was Igor, and on another was Von Goosewing. To be more accurate, Von Goosewing was stuck to the chair by the glue-like flour and water mixture!

'We've sure rounded up a lot of pests!' sneered Ed. 'Only one left is that ridiculous duck!'

'He'll show up!' grinned Mitch. 'Then we'll deal with him good an' proper!'

Von Goosewing attempted to wriggle around on his sticky chair. He was so angry he simply couldn't keep still. 'Dealing wiz Dugula is my prerogative!' he snapped. 'I am zee wampire-hunter und I demand zat I haff zee satisfaction of destroying zee monster!'

Ed glared at the doctor, who began to cringe and cower slightly. 'You demand satisfaction do you, Doctor Dough? Well, I think it'll satisfy me to clean all that sticky mess off you by throwing you in the duckpond right *now*!'

'Nein! Nein!' screamed Von Goosewing, as he was carried out by the villainous partners and flung in the pond. The whole procedure took only a couple of minutes – not long enough for the others to escape!

Ignorant of everyone else's misfortune, the happy Duckula found the broken rope ladder and made his way back into the library. He'd waited a little while behind the bookshelves and listened carefully to make sure Von Goosewing wasn't still there.

His next destination was the bedroom with the four-poster bed. Once there, he searched for the source of the chink of light in the hidden room. It wasn't a loose floorboard; carpets covered the floor.

Could the furniture provide a clue, he thought, looking at the heavy, antique dressing table. A closer look supplied the answer! The floor at the back of the dressing table wasn't carpeted and there was a big gap in the floorboards! So that was it! Things, valuable and worthless, had been falling down over hundreds of years. Poor, innocent Sam had been banished because of a silly floorboard!

Humming with happiness and pride, Duckula went to find the others. Now that he'd really solved the mystery he was so excited that he hardly considered the danger from his enemies. It was quite light now, so he decided to go into the gallery to get a good view of anyone who might be down in the great hall.

What he didn't expect was to see everyone in the great hall – except Von Goosewing, who was in the duckpond! One peep was enough to tell Duckula what had happened. The horrible Mitch and Ed were holding Nanny, Igor and Charlie captive!

Mitch's gruff voice broke the silence. 'We'd better do something with this gang before the newspaper nosy parkers come round to see that duck! The duckpond's a bit too obvious – and it's occupied at the moment! Let's lock 'em in the cellars till we decide what to do with 'em!'

'Great idea!' said Ed.

'*Without* food or water, naturally!'

'Oh, you're '*orrid*!' squealed Nanny.

Igor, who, in different circumstances might have enjoyed a spell in the cellars, was furious and poor Charlie looked as if he was about to cry!

Duckula, watching from the gallery, didn't know what to do to help.

Then some amazing events began to happen! It was really a sort of chain reaction set off by the electronic warning system, which Duckula had retrieved from Nanny, starting to make its usual high-pitched noise.

Oh no, thought Duckula, as everyone in the hall looked up, startled.

Then whoosh! With a sudden, explosive burst, the large and varied collection of plants in the gallery grew and grew! In a matter of seconds, Duckula was lifted up by an expanding plant which had previously been standing harmlessly behind him. The plant grew swiftly, its leaves spreading out over the edge of the gallery. Stunned, Duckula was thrown out into space!

'Help!' he cried, as he flew through the air and caught hold of the enormous chandelier.

Swinging from one side of the hall to the other, he was reminded of swashbuckling scenes in those old movies. He'd often imagined himself doing something like this . . . but imagining was one thing. Being pushed by a plant was another!

There was a sickening creaking noise. Duckula realised that the chandelier was about to crash to the ground. 'Nanny, Igor, Charlie . . . move away, quickly!' he cried as he leapt on to the top of a tall dresser.

'We're off!' yelled the terrified Mitch. 'We've had enough!'

But as the cowardly pair scattered, the main doors opened to reveal the newspaper reporters.

'Catch them!' yelled Duckula.

So Duckula became a hero, not for spending the night alone in a haunted house, for, as you know, he wasn't alone at all!

He was a hero for far better reasons than that! After all, he brought two rogues to justice, cleared Sam's name and found the lost deeds of Windup Manor, as well as lots more valuables belonging to the Windup family. Which meant that Lady Windup could start her plant project!

Everyone praised his daring and courage – especially Nanny! And he received the prize money, so he was able to afford to pay for his electronics set *and* still have cash left over for milkshakes! He even bought Nanny and Igor presents!

Spare a thought for Von Goosewing! I hope he gets out of that duckpond before the next Duckula story!

By the way, I wonder just who was playing that violin . . .?

Goodbye out there – whatever you are!

Sheep Ahoy!

GRAHAM MARKS AND CHRISTOPHER MAYNARD

A hilarious collection of extraordinary but absolutely true stories – stranger than fiction – culled from the back pages and people columns of newspapers.

£1.95　☐

Mispronts

GRAHAM MARKS AND CHRISTOPHER MAYNARD

An amusing selection of silly misprints from newspapers and magazines.

£1.95　☐

Odd Pets

GRAHAM MARKS AND CHRISTOPHER MAYNARD

A useful collection of outlandish pets, specially compiled for the lazy pet owner who is not excited by the idea of cleaning out, grooming and feeding. All of the pets to be found in this book are easily obtained, either from the wild, or the human body, and require the minimum of care and maintenance.

£1.95　☐

ARMADA

Crazy Curriculum
JONATHAN CLEMENTS

A hilarious alternative look at school education, including study notes on traditional subjects such as history, and not so usual ones such as human behaviour. There are also exam papers and answers, quizzes, timetables and school reports of famous people.

£1.95 ☐

Writing Jokes and Riddles
BILL HOWARD

This is a joke book with a difference – it actually teaches you how to make up a joke! Interspersed with plenty of hilarious examples it also contains a list of key words on which most jokes are based.

£1.95 ☐

Yeuuch!
PETE SAUNDERS

A collection of revolting, horrible and disgusting things you'll wish you'd never discovered that will appeal to those who delight in gruesome detail. All the facts are true and many are highlighted by clever, zany illustrations.

£1.95 ☐

ARMADA

All these books are available at your local bookshop or newsagent, or can be ordered from the publisher. To order direct from the publishers just tick the title you want and fill in the form below:

Name _____

Address _____

_____

Send to: Collins Childrens Cash Sales
PO Box 11
Falmouth
Cornwall
TR10 9EN

Please enclose a cheque or postal order or debit my Visa/Access –

Credit card no:

Expiry date:

Signature:

– to the value of the cover price plus:

UK: 60p for the first book, 25p for the second book, plus 15p per copy for each additional book ordered to a maximum charge of £1.90.

BFPO: 60p for the first book, 25p for the second book plus 15p per copy for the next 7 books, thereafter 9p per book.

Overseas and Eire: £1.25 for the first book, 75p for the second book. Thereafter 28p per book.

ARMADA